SIGNET

REGENCY ROMANCE

April Kihlstrom

The Wily Wastrel

D0030508

DON'T MISS THE OTHER ENCHANTING
REGENCIES BY APRIL KIHLSTROM

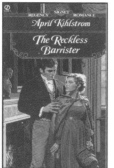

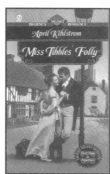

ISBN 0-451-19820-4

US $4.99 / CAN $6.99

50499

EAN

from SIGNET

A SCANDALOUS PROPOSAL

There was a look of thunder on George's face, and it only darkened when he spied Miss Galsworth sitting in James's carriage. "What the devil are you doing here? And at such an hour of the morning?" James demanded of his brother.

Lord Darton glared at him. "When you did not return yesterday with Miss Galsworth, her family sent for me. I shall not soon forgive you for placing me in such an untenable position!"

Mrs. Galsworth and a man James presumed to be Mr. Galsworth were in the drawing room. At the sight of her daughter, the woman gave a tiny cry of relief.

"What have you done to our Juliet?" the older man demanded.

James looked at Miss Galsworth and said, "Juliet?"

She nodded.

George asked in disbelief, "You spent the night with the girl and didn't even learn her name?"

"What the devil do you intend to do to make this right?" Mr. Galsworth demanded.

James looked at Miss Galsworth, smiled wryly and half-apologetically to her, and said, with a calm he was very far from feeling, "Miss Galsworth and I shall be married, of course. As soon as possible."

Juliet's eyes were wide, and she stared at him in disbelief. . . .

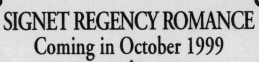

The Wily Wastrel

April Kihlstrom

A SIGNET BOOK

SIGNET
Published by New American Library, a division of
Penguin Putnam Inc., 375 Hudson Street,
New York, New York 10014, U.S.A.
Penguin Books Ltd, 27 Wrights Lane,
London W8 5TZ, England
Penguin Books Australia Ltd, Ringwood,
Victoria, Australia
Penguin Books Canada Ltd, 10 Alcorn Avenue,
Toronto, Ontario, Canada M4V 3B2
Penguin Books (N.Z.) Ltd, 182–190 Wairau Road,
Auckland 10, New Zealand

Penguin Books Ltd, Registered Offices:
Harmondsworth, Middlesex, England

First published by Signet, an imprint of New American Library,
a division of Penguin Putnam Inc.

First Printing, October 1999
10 9 8 7 6 5 4 3 2 1

Prologue

⌒

James Langford, known to the *ton* as an engaging but thoroughly hopeless wastrel who gambled and danced and spent far too much time and energy on his clothes and nothing more, quirked an eyebrow at the man looking at his work.

"Well?" he asked in a brisk voice that none of his friends would have recognized. "Will it do?"

The man nodded. "Aye, it'll more than do." He paused and stared at James. "Why the devil do you waste your time playing at being such a frivolous fellow when you can build machines like this?"

But this was too much for James. He fixed the fellow with a piercing stare and said, coolly, "You forget, sir, that I am a gentleman."

The other man snorted in disgust. "Bleeding gentlemen! Worthless lot of creatures! And you choose to be one of 'em? Pack of nonsense! It's not my business to say so, I suppose, but I can't see why you would."

"You are quite right, it is not your business," James agreed austerely. "Will you be taking the machine with you now, or sending for it later?" he asked.

The man sighed again. "Oh, I'll send for it. My man will be here in the morning with a wagon to transport the thing to my factory up north. He'll bring a bank draft with him, as usual."

He paused, then held out his hand as he added, with

an apologetic grin, "I meant no offense, Langford. It's just that I like you, and that's not something as I'd say about or to most gentlemen."

James took the offered hand and he smiled a wry, oddly sweet smile of his own as he replied, "No offense taken, sir. There are even moments when I'd agree with you. But for now I am as I am. Meanwhile, I'll arrange to have my man waiting to give yours a hand loading this machine onto your wagon in the morning. And now," he said, reaching for the candelabra, "we'd best go. I'm supposed to be at a gaming party and it wouldn't do for me to be more than fashionably late."

Another snort, this time a gentler one, was the other man's only answer.

Chapter 1

James Langford, younger brother of Lord Darton, returned Miss Merriweather to her mother's loving care and looked about him for another partner. Already there were a number of young ladies trying to catch his eye.

His satin coat of soft blue echoed an earlier age, far different from the simple black or other dark colors worn by most gentlemen those days. But none of the ladies were heard to cavil at his taste. Indeed, they were more likely to admire the clocking on his stockings than to call it out of fashion.

Langford was not unaware of the stir he was causing and he wondered, idly, what would happen if he were to go so far as to powder his hair. The smile that tilted up the corners of his mouth at the thought caused more than one young lady to hope he was thinking of her.

Even as he steeled himself to find another partner, a friend grabbed Langford by the arm and said, "You must see this quiz. Don't know what the girl's mother was thinking! She squints, positively squints. And not a fortune in sight to make it all acceptable. Or so they say. At least, thank God, there is no whiff of trade about her or the girl would be done for entirely!"

James allowed himself to be commandeered. Why not, after all? He had nothing more amusing to do.

Still, it was not amusement he felt as he looked in the direction Farnsworth pointed him. He saw, as promised, a young lady who indeed was something of a quiz.

"Her dress don't in the least become her," Farnsworth said.

Langford had to agree. "And her expression," he noted, "seems calculated to warn off anyone foolish enough to think of asking her to dance."

"As if they would!" Farnsworth snorted in disgust. "Just look at that simpering woman beside her. Obviously the girl's mother."

James sighed. There was a hint of sympathy in his voice as he said, "Poor creature. It's no wonder she's become fodder for malicious gossip."

"What was her mother thinking to clad such a sturdy young woman in frothy white?" Farnsworth persisted. "Or to have her auburn hair cropped so short? It only draws attention to her squint!"

"What, indeed?" James murmured. "Poor creature. Thank heavens she is not related to me. Otherwise I might feel compelled to ask her to dance."

Farnsworth shuddered at the thought. He and Langford were about to turn away when she looked at them. James stopped, transfixed. There was intelligence and even wry humor in those eyes. And understanding of precisely what he and all the other gawkers must be thinking.

Before he knew what he was about, before he could even think to alter course, Langford found himself moving toward the girl and bowing to her mother. He didn't know the woman but he knew one of the women beside her.

"Lady Batten, would you be so kind as to introduce me to this young lady?"

Lady Batten gaped at him and then smiled tightly, as though at some private joke. "Of course. Miss Galsworth, may I present Mr. Langford. Mr. Langford, Miss Galsworth. And her mother, Mrs. Galsworth."

James bowed again. He felt a strong sense of impending doom, worsened by the way Mrs. Galsworth looked at him with such a satisfied gleam in her eye. Nor was he reassured when he turned to Miss Galsworth and she took his outstretched hand with what could only be patent relief in her eyes.

When her fingers clutched at his, as though at a lifeline, James wondered if he had made a horrible mistake. As he led her toward the other dancers, however, Miss Galsworth surprised him.

In a voice pitched low enough to carry to his ears only she said, "I am well aware, sir, that you have the power to bring any young lady into fashion with your attention. While I do not hope for more than mere tolerance, I shall not forget your kindness in asking me to dance."

And then she smiled at him. That smiled changed everything. With a shock, James realized that Miss Galsworth had the potential to be very pretty. If it weren't for her horrid hairstyle and appalling gown.

But the smile was gone as swiftly as it had appeared and she was the plain creature with a squint once again. James did his best to banish the other image from his mind.

Still, they took their places and he smiled at her whenever the figures of the dance brought them together. He made certain to engage her in unexceptionable conversation that others could overhear. To his great relief, Miss Galsworth neither simpered nor showed an unbecoming forwardness nor was she afflicted by shyness.

By the time the music drew to a close, James was feeling quite pleased with himself. He knew he was kindhearted and he was well aware of his own power in society. Smug in his sense of having done a good deed, he escorted Miss Galsworth back to her mother.

That would have been the end of things if she had not said lightly, as though it were inconsequential, "Why did you ask me to dance, Mr. Langford? Was it a wager? Or am I one of your charity cases?"

That caused James to miss a step and he nearly stumbled. He gaped at Miss Galsworth but quickly shut his open mouth. He would not allow her to provoke him. Grimly he said, "You ought not to ask such questions! They impugn both my motives and your own good qualities."

"Oh, but I have no good qualities," she replied frankly. "At least, nothing that would recommend me to so notable a dandy as yourself."

"I am not a dandy!"

She hesitated, studied him carefully, then nodded. "No? Well, perhaps not. Your shirt points are not ridiculously high after all, though the, er, uniqueness of your coat might make one wonder. Forgive me. I have nothing to recommend me to so notable a *gentleman* as yourself."

He wanted to deny her self-deprecations. And certainly James was an accomplished enough flirt that he ought to have found it easy enough to do so. But when he looked at Miss Galsworth, he discovered he could not lie to those clear green eyes.

A smile twitched at the corners of her mouth. "I thought so," she said. "A charity case. I only asked about the wager because I knew you to be a notable gamester. But not about this sort of thing, I would guess."

"You guess correctly," James said, his voice tight with disapproval.

She sighed. "Now I have offended you and I did not mean to do so. Not after you have been so kind to me. I am sorry, Mr. Langford."

Suddenly his anger melted away. How could he remain angry at a girl who spoke so bluntly, who played no simpering games with him? It was such a refreshing change from all the rest of the year's crop that he almost committed the solecism of asking Miss Galsworth whence she had sprung.

Instead he smiled again, returned her to her mother without risking another, possibly dangerous conversation, and bowed fully intending to simply walk away.

Mrs. Galsworth had other plans.

"You will come to call on us, won't you, Mr. Langford? Your mother and I were bosom bows."

James doubted it sincerely. But he could not call the woman a liar to her face and his mother was dead so he could not ask her to refute the outrageous claim. All he could do was bow again, smile noncommittally, and attempt to beat as hasty a retreat as possible.

Mrs. Galsworth would have stopped him, but now that James had danced with her daughter, other gentlemen decided to be as brave and her attention was claimed by them.

James slipped away and headed for the gaming rooms. He hated to gamble, but no one could have guessed it by his demeanor. And for once, the gaming rooms felt like a refuge. Besides, having just earned a hefty commission, he had to account for his good fortune somehow. Best to let the *ton,* and his brother George, believe he had won it at cards.

Unfortunately, events seemed to conspire against the small measure of peace James had made with the secret way in which he made his fortune and flouted convention. Almost the first conversation he joined seemed like a reproach.

"Heard about Kellingham?" Beardsley demanded.

"Married the daughter of a shipping magnate, didn't he?" someone else replied.

"Perhaps he, er, needed to recoup the family fortune," James suggested mildly. "And I've heard nothing to say against the girl's father."

"Except that he owns a damned shipping yard!" Beardsley snorted.

"Would it have been better for Kellingham to lose the land his family has owned for generations?" a third gentleman countered. "I've heard that was the alternative if the merchant had not come up to scratch."

"Well, no," Cathcart conceded. "But that does not mean we have to like it."

"I thank God none of our families have had to face such a choice and been tainted by the smell of trade," someone sniffed disdainfully.

"Mind you," Cathcart said to James, "your brother's wife does interest herself in some of the oddest things."

James went very still. His eyes narrowed. In a voice that was dangerously soft he asked, "Are you impugning Lady Darton, sir?"

He knew full well the fellow did not mean Athenia, that paragon of conventionality. He knew full well it was Philip's wife who trod the line toward eccentricity. But nevertheless James watched in satisfaction as Cathcart sputtered and hastily withdrew the gibe.

Someone else turned the subject to safer matters and James suppressed the sigh of relief he felt. Confound it, what would the *ton* say, what would they do if they ever found out that Philip and Emily owned a mill? So far his brother had managed to keep the thing a secret but there was always the risk of discovery. As there was with his own activities.

James would have liked to leave the game at once, the room no longer feeling like a refuge to him. But he could not do so. Not without drawing unwelcome attention to his reaction to the conversation and unhealthy speculation once he was gone. So, for the moment, he stayed.

Two hours later, James rose from the card tables in disbelief. He had won. Actually won! It was a most unusual circumstance. Oh, he had had short runs of luck before, and one of his talents was pretending it was often so. But the truth was, James rarely won like this.

"Perhaps Miss Galsworth has brought you good fortune tonight, Langford," Beardsley suggested with a wicked gleam in his eye.

"Heard you've a command to call upon the gel tomorrow," Cathcart added with a grin.

James eyed them both with disfavor. "How the devil did you hear about that in here?" he demanded.

The two men shrugged. "One simply does," Beardsley replied.

"Yes, well, I asked her to dance. Once. And that is the end of it," James retorted.

"Of course, m'boy, of course," Cathcart replied.

James pressed his lips together in a thin line, well aware that further protests would only make matters worse. He bowed to his friends and stalked from the card room.

He made his way toward the door, determined to leave before any other unfortunate girl could catch his eye or make a claim on his kindness. Had his attention not been so thoroughly engaged in his plans to escape, James might well have noticed the Galsworth party in time to sheer away. As it was, he almost ran into Mrs. Galsworth and he did trod on the hem of Miss Galsworth's gown. Everyone nearby heard the sound as the flounce at the hem of her dress tore under his clumsy foot.

James turned red and started to stammer an apology. Mrs. Galsworth started to ring a peal over the offender and stopped the moment she recognized who it was. Miss Galsworth turned first a fiery red and then went very pale. It was she who spoke first.

"Never mind, Mama. It doesn't signify. We were leaving anyway. Let us go out to the carriage. It must be waiting by now. I am certain Mr. Langford meant no harm."

Mrs. Galsworth smiled thinly and tapped him playfully on the arm with her fan. "I shall forgive Mr. Langford," she said, an arch note to her voice, "if he promises, without fail, to call upon us tomorrow!"

James could only bow. He would not, he vowed silently, promise such a thing. And yet neither would he cause any further commotion by refusing aloud to do so.

Fortunately, Mrs. Galsworth took his bow as an assent, as he meant her to do. Miss Galsworth was not so easily deceived. She cast an ironical smile his way and then swept her mother away.

For some reason, her perceptiveness disturbed James. And he found himself absurdly wishing he could explain.

"Dashed odd girl," said Farnsworth, who had suddenly appeared at his elbow. "Best stay until you're certain her party is gone, otherwise bound to find yourself pounced upon all over again."

"I suspect you might be right," James agreed. "I think I shall go and find our hostess. I'll take my leave of her, and by the time I reach the door, the way should be clear."

"Come with you," Farnsworth suggested. "I can help fend them off, if need be!"

James laughed. "It shan't come to that," he said, with a shake of his head.

Farnsworth disagreed. "Do a kindness for a plain gel and you're never rid of her, Langford. Just look at my cousin Lydia. Wore her fiancé down 'til he had to ask her to marry him."

With pardonable exasperation in his voice James said indignantly, "I only asked the girl to dance! Once. And that's the start and end of it."

"We'll see," was Farnsworth's gloomy reply.

James shook his head again. Still, by the time he had reached home and parted company with Farnsworth, he felt a distinct sense of relief at having somehow escaped a horrible fate. He would not, definitely not, call upon the Galsworth girl on the morrow.

James would have been aghast had he known that at the town house her mother had hired for the Season, Miss Galsworth was sitting by the window, brushing her curls, and thinking of him. He would have been even more appalled had he known she was reliving, over and over again, the experience of dancing with him.

He might even have felt compelled to flee London for a spell and that would have been a pity. For that would have robbed the *ton* of what was about to become their biggest amusement of the Season.

Chapter 2

In the drawing room, as they waited for callers, Mrs. Galsworth studied her daughter carefully. "I do not know what to do with you, Juliet," she said, shaking her head in patent disapproval. "You have no social graces. You will never be known for your beauty. You do not even have the proper accomplishments to recommend you to a gentleman. How are we ever going to marry you off?"

Juliet looked away. There was an edge of hurt in her voice as she replied, "You need not catalogue my faults, Mama. I know them only too well. No seam that I sew ever runs straight. No music that I play will ever do other than hurt the ears of anyone nearby enough to hear. I dance, but only the kindest of gentlemen would pretend to call me graceful."

Indeed, Juliet thought, she could well have been said to be the despair of a mother who had dreamed, when naming her, of a dainty daughter, with a heart-shaped face, who would float along, the epitome of femininity. The jest, of course, was on her mother.

As she had often been heard to say, somewhat bitterly, to Mr. Galsworth, "The daughter of the gamekeeper seems more like a lady than Juliet!"

"I try, Mama," she said now, hoping to turn aside her mother's anger. "I truly do. I try to glide across the floor, the way my dancing instructor has demonstrated. And I practice every day on the pianoforte. Indeed I have even used the recipe you gave me for Unction de Maintenon for the removal of freckles."

"And none of it to any avail!" her mother retorted sharply. "You remain as you are: a clumsy, unmusical, freckle-faced girl. Your only talent is working with your hands and heaven help us if anyone ever finds out! Why, oh, why, if you must work with your hands, can you not learn to use a needle? That would be unexceptionable. But no, you must needs interest yourself in all sorts of unfeminine things."

Mrs. Galsworth shuddered and Juliet could stand no more. "Would it have been better if I had left the pump broken?" she demanded. "So that we would have had no water until someone else could have been found to fix it? Or not repaired the mangle in the laundry shed so that our clothes remained dirty? And perhaps you would have preferred that I had not fixed that carriage wheel? Perhaps you would have preferred if I had let it come off and we had all found ourselves tumbled into the ditch?"

Mrs. Galsworth could not meet her daughter's eyes. "It is just so unfeminine," she said. "It makes you seem such an odd creature. Your governess should never have allowed you to poke your nose into every corner of the estate and watch as all manner of things were being fixed."

"Papa said it was handy having someone about like me," Juliet said hopefully.

"Handy?" Mrs. Galsworth screeched. "Handy? And do you suppose any gentleman is wishing for someone handy when he looks about him for a wife? Do you suppose he wishes to know she can rescue him, should their carriage begin to fail? Or that she can repair the kitchen pump?"

"No, Mama, I suppose not," Juliet replied meekly. But it was not enough to turn her mother's wrath.

Having begun a catalogue of Juliet's faults, she could not help but continue.

"The moment we arrived here, you prowled from top to bottom looking for things you could fix. Do you know how much I have had to increase the wages of the entire staff to ensure that none of them speak of this to anyone outside the house? Do you realize that even so we cannot be entirely certain they will not?"

"Yes, Mama."

With tears of frustration in her eyes, Mrs. Galsworth tugged at Juliet's dress, trying to make it drape in a more flattering way. "Do try to behave yourself today. We must hope that at least some gentlemen will come to call. Perhaps Mr. Langford. He seemed taken with you last night. Here, hold this piece of needlework and pretend you are sewing."

Juliet tried to refuse. "But it is a lie!"

"Everything is a lie," her mother countered. "At least when one is trying to find a husband and bring him up to scratch. After you are married you may do as you please, but for now you must pretend to be an unexceptionable young lady! The Lord knows you will have to lie to do that!"

It was impossible, thought Juliet. Her dress of soft, pale-green muslin would have looked lovely on a dainty young thing. On her it looked hideous, or so she supposed. Whatever had possessed her mother to insist upon the knots of ribbons and roses all over the skirt and bodice? Or tell the maid to thread a matching ribbon through her short curls? And why on earth had she agreed?

For peace, Juliet thought gloomily. Just as, for peace, she would hold the abominable needlework in her hands. And hope that she did not prick herself with the needle just as some gentleman entered the room! As if it would matter, she chided herself. She could not imagine that any young man would actually come to call. Or that if he did, it was with any serious interest in herself.

"Don't you wish to be married?" Mrs. Galsworth demanded, her shrill voice penetrating Juliet's reverie.

"I, of course I do," Juliet replied. Then, stiffly she added, "I daresay I have indulged in as many daydreams and fantasies on the subject as any other young lady. It is just that I look at myself with a clear and unjaundiced eye, Mama, and I can see how unlikely it is that any of my daydreams will ever come to pass."

"You are hopeless," Mrs. Galsworth said, shaking her head, "hopeless."

But there was no more time to quarrel. The first two gentlemen had arrived. Unfortunately, it was clear to Juliet that they had come to gawk and take back tales with which to regale their friends. She was hard put to be polite to them, but under her mother's stern gaze she tried.

Two other gentlemen were kind but aroused not the least interest in Juliet's breast, and it was only when the last of the callers for the day were gone that she could admit to herself there was only one gentleman she wished to see. And he had not come.

"I do not understand it!" her mother said querulously. "Mr. Langford promised to call upon us today."

Juliet tilted up her chin. "I, for one, am glad he did not come," she lied. "He is everything I disdain. He is an indolent dandy who does nothing with his time save worry about his clothes, gossip, gamble, and no doubt, chase after women. He lives, they say, upon two things: the generosity of his older brother, Lord Darton, and upon the funds that he has won gambling. No, Mama, I am grateful he did not come today."

"You are hopeless, Juliet, hopeless," was her mother's only answer.

Juliet turned away, her thoughts still on Mr. Langford. For all her harsh words, she could not help but recall that when he had asked her to dance, when he had talked with her, it had seemed to her as if there was a rare intelligence in his eyes, an understanding in his expression, a kindred spirit in his soul.

It was all nonsense; of course it was. And yet, Juliet wished he had called today, as promised. Perhaps then she could have dismissed him as an indolent dandy and given her thoughts a more rational direction.

But Mr. Langford did not call. And because he did not, he only found a securer foothold in Juliet's thoughts and in her heart.

In his bachelor rooms on the other side of town, Mr. James Langford was writing to his brother Philip's mill manager. He was explaining to the man precisely how to adjust the looms he had sent to the factory some months before.

It was just the sort of thing James enjoyed and he ought to have been feeling quite content as he alternated between writing and sipping the coffee at his elbow.

But he wasn't content. As he had the night before, James worried about Philip today. Again he wondered how long they could keep his ownership of the mill a secret.

Perhaps it could be passed off as mere eccentricity, but that was not a very satisfactory solution. Particularly if George, Lord Darton, were to find out. How they had come to have such a high stickler for a brother James never had been able to comprehend.

Speaking of George, James wondered what he would think of Miss Galsworth. Which led to wondering what she was doing and whether anyone had come to call upon her today. And whether she was still expecting him.

Abruptly realizing what he was doing, James took a deep breath and tried to turn the direction of his thoughts. He was resolute in his determination not to call upon her today. Why, after all, should he?

Simply because Mrs. Galsworth claimed to have been bosom bows with his mother? He thought it most unlikely. Or because Miss Galsworth might be expecting him? Absurd! She had known he asked her to dance only to be kind and surely she was too intelligent to believe he owed her anything more?

But James could not shake her image. Why had such an intelligent girl allowed herself to be dressed up in such a way? It was not, he would swear, that she was a meek creature who dared not speak back to her parents. And she quite evidently realized what a quiz of a figure she presented. There must be more to it than that and he wondered what it might be.

Even as James was muttering to himself about Miss Galsworth, his older brother, George, was shown in to the study. Lord Darton looked about the room and then fixed a disapproving gaze upon his brother. He eyed with particular disapproval the bright yellow coat that James was wearing. Still that was not the matter of which he spoke.

"I do not understand, James, why you cannot instruct your servants to keep this place in order."

"They are not allowed in here," James replied mildly.

"That I can well believe!" Darton said with a snort of disgust. "And if anyone were to see this room, they would have great difficulty reconciling it with their notions of you. I have trouble reconciling it! You are always so fastidious in your dress. How can you abide such clutter?"

"I like it," James said with a singularly sweet smile. "Come, sit, and cease to rip up at me. One would think you had never been in this room before. Or that you would at least think of a new speech to give when you ring that particular peal over my head."

Darton sat. "Look here, James," he said, "you are

four and twenty and it is time you changed your ways."

"It is not your place to tell me how to live my life," James said with a stiffness he could not hold back.

"Perhaps not," George conceded, "but I am your brother and therefore entitled to feel concern for you. The fact that I supply you with an allowance is a small matter that might also weigh with you—if you felt the sort of family affection and gratitude you ought to feel."

James ignored this gibe. Twisting a writing quill in his hand, he said, "So you think I ought to change my way of life. Is there any particular manner in which you wish me to change it?"

George hesitated. He avoided meeting his brother's eyes. "Well, er, that is, you are perhaps of an age to think of setting up a nursery."

"Without a wife?" James asked, with pretend surprise. "George, I am shocked at you, positively shocked!"

Stung, Lord Darton snapped, "You know very well that I mean you should marry first, James, and then set up your nursery!"

"And have you, er, set your eyes on a suitable prospect?" James asked with a carelessness he did not feel.

"Yes. No. That is, Athenia and I thought we ought to find out if you had."

"Me?" James was taken aback. "What on earth would give you the notion . . . "

Abruptly his voice trailed off. After a moment he said, "Miss Galsworth?"

"Just so." George nodded. He tried to look innocent and failed miserably. Finally he said, "Oh the devil with it! Athenia insisted that I visit you and find out what your interest is in the girl. Athenia heard, from one of her bosom bows, that you have taken up some nobody from the country who has shockingly poor taste in clothes, does not know how to arrange her hair, and positively squints. At least I think those were Athenia's words. And why you should do so if you had not set your thoughts on settling down is more than either of us can imagine."

James almost laughed at his brother's confusion. But he didn't. If there was one quality George lacked, and in truth there were many, it was a sense of humor. Instead he answered in a quiet, calm voice.

"I danced one dance with Miss Galsworth, nothing more. I felt sorry for her and thought perhaps it would help the poor girl if I did so. But that is the beginning and the end of things."

Darton nodded. "Well, that's a relief. I rather hoped Athenia had gotten it wrong. You, of all people, to be taken in by a quiz of a gel in shocking clothes. Preposterous! And so I told Athenia."

James felt something stir within his breast. An instinctive protest perhaps. A desire to tell his brother that it was not such a preposterous notion after all. But that would never do. George would feel it his duty to interfere. Or rather Athenia would. And between them they would cut up his peace and probably Miss Galworth's as well. No, best to say nothing more.

George rose to his feet, a satisfied look on his face, his duty patently fulfilled. "Care to join me for dinner at the club?" he asked.

James shook his head.

"Gaming, are you?"

No, but as an excuse it would do. James nodded.

George frowned and sat down again, a stern look upon his face and grim lines around his mouth. He looked as though he had just remembered something. He had. That became clear the moment he began to speak.

"This has to stop," Darton said harshly.

"What has to stop?" James asked warily.

George waved a hand. "This . . . this gaming!" He paused and drew in a breath. "You may as well tell me the extent of your debts, for I have no doubt I shall soon be called upon to settle them.''

James was taken aback. Where the devil had this notion come from? Cautiously he tried to feel his way. "Actually, George, I am rather beforehand with the world, at the moment. Indeed, just last night I won a tidy sum at Lady Merriweather's party.''

Lord Darton waved his hand again, this time dismissively. "The merest trifle,'' he said impatiently. "Or so I heard. Come, tell me the truth, James! From what I've heard, you have had some grand losses and some minor wins. What are your debts? You need not fear to tell me. I may scold but I promise I shall settle them. Don't want m'brother falling into the hands of cents-per-centers.''

"I have no debts," James repeated, unable to keep the edge out of his voice.

George gaped at him. "No debts? Come now, James, that's doing it much too brown! You forget, I am the one who makes you your allowance and I know full well it does not run to the kind of clothes you wear or the upkeep of these rooms. Not when you are losing as much as I have heard you lost these past few weeks.''

James sighed and closed his eyes. He wanted, desperately, to tell his brother how he was making his money. But he knew too well how George would react. Bad enough that Philip was a barrister! To be making money, as he was, almost as though he were in trade, would draw more disapproval from Lord Darton than he wished to deal with just now. Or ever.

He opened his eyes and shrugged. "Believe what you will, brother," James said, "I have no debts.''

George smacked the flat of his hand on James's desk. "Dash it all, James! If you don't need funds, it must mean you've been gambling in some godforsaken gaming hell! And winning. For the moment. And I've no doubt you believe it will continue forever. But it won't!"

Lord Darton began to pace about the room. "You're an intelligent man, James. You must realize they think you a pigeon ripe for the plucking and plan to do so the moment you let down your guard. They must believe I'll back your debts. So they are letting you win. For the moment. But once you become accustomed to gambling large sums, you'll suddenly find your luck changing. You'll go down to the tune of hundreds or perhaps even thousands of pounds, I'll wager."

He paused and stared grimly at his younger brother. In a stern, indeed quite fatherly voice, Darton said, "If you allow that to happen, James, I swear that will be the end of your allowance. I swear I'll send you to live on my Yorkshire estate. I'll not stand for a wastrel of a brother who hasn't the sense to stay out of gaming hells! And don't try to tell me that's not where you're gambling because I know full well how your luck has been running when you play in respectable homes."

James did not try to tell his brother a thing. Instead he tried to make light of matters. A tiny smile quirked at the corners of his mouth as he said, "I promise you, George, you shan't have to rescue me from my debts. Nor," he added, holding up a hand to forestall his brother's next fear, "will I resort to cents-per-centers. I know too well the danger there."

Lord Darton tried to stare down his brother, but it was hopeless. James merely smiled at him with that impassive expression he used to such excellent effect.

Finally George gave another snort of disgust and turned toward the door. "Very well," he said. "Have it your way. Just don't cry to me when you find yourself in the River Tick. I mean what I say. I'll cover your debts but you will find yourself on my estate in Yorkshire."

And with that, Lord Darton left. James watched

him go and thought, inconsequentially, that it wouldn't
be such a terrible thing to be on the estate in Yorkshire. No one would bother him and he could tinker
to his heart's content.

Ah, but then he would be away from his friends in
London and the men here who were as eager to try
new things, to experiment, as he was.

There was even, he thought with a wry smile, a part
of him that liked to go to balls and pretend to be
an indolent dandy. He could not, mind you, entirely
reconcile it with the serious side of his nature. But
then, he was too easygoing to even try.

Before he knew it, James's thoughts were once
more on Miss Galsworth as he imagined how she
might look if he had the dressing of her and could
determine how her hair should be cut. He even
thought that perhaps, away from the crowded ball-
room, she might be able to speak with some sense!

Chapter 3

$\backsim$

He was not going to call on Miss Galsworth. Of course he was not. James told himself so, over and over again. Unfortunately he did not listen. Which was why, early the next afternoon, he found himself standing on her doorstep.

He was not entirely pleased to see several other gentlemen mount the steps ahead of him. Even though he knew they were probably there because he had first set the fashion by dancing with Miss Galsworth.

And he knew that it was to be expected that some gentlemen would call the day after the ball. But two days later? James felt an irrational pique as he was shown into the drawing room. Particularly since he could not say that there had been any noticeable improvement in Miss Galsworth's appearance.

Today she wore a light blue gown covered with ruffles and a blue ribbon that pulled her hair back in a way that was even more unflattering than the manner in which it had been dressed for the ball. On her lap was a piece of needlework, which she eyed, from time to time, with patent disfavor.

Clearly she was a young lady who had no hope, barring a secret fortune that no one knew of, of ever forming an eligible attachment to a member of the *ton*. If she were to marry at all, her parents would have to swallow their pride, ignore the disdain of the *ton,* and look for the son of a wealthy merchant who wished to improve his station in life. And even then she might not find the matter an easy one to bring off.

Or so James was telling himself as he bowed to Mrs. Galsworth. But then he turned to Miss Galsworth and she smiled at him. A genuine smile that lit up her face and brought depth to her really very pretty green eyes.

Without thinking, James fashioned a matching smile on his face. And as he bowed, he found himself seeking out the chair nearest to her own.

"How do you do, Miss Galsworth?"

She regarded him with wry amusement that she did not trouble to hide. Before she could answer him, however, her mother did so.

"You were to have come yesterday, Mr. Langford! How naughty of you to make us wait."

James regarded Mrs. Galsworth with disfavor. His voice was cool and his eyebrows arched in polite disdain as he replied, "When you invited me to call 'to-morrow' as you put it, the time was after midnight. Naturally I assumed you meant today."

That put her in her place. It was not well done of James but the woman irritated him beyond measure. Several of the gentleman gaped at him, having rarely heard James be rude to a hostess before.

But at his side a soft voice murmured, "Bravo! You have routed Mama and that is not easily done."

He looked at her swiftly but Miss Galsworth's face gave away nothing. It was as if she had never spoken. Still, there was a hint of mischief in her eyes that found an answering spark within his own and he found to his surprise that he wanted to draw it out even more.

"Would you care to go for a drive in the park, later this afternoon, Miss Galsworth?" he asked.

"No," was the cool reply.

Then, before James could recover from his astonishment at the refusal, she added, a smile twitching at the corners of her mouth, "But I should like to visit a lending library, if you would take me."

Mrs. Galsworth audibly gasped at her daughter's effrontery. Hastily she tried to mend matters. "My dear, I can go to Hookham's and retrieve any novel you wish," she said.

Miss Galsworth continued to look at James, a patent challenge in her eyes as she said, "I should rather go with Mr. Langford."

He was amused. "Shall I call for you at four?" he asked.

She nodded and he wondered if it was fear or eagerness he read in her expression. Either way, James was curious enough now to be glad he had extended his impulsive invitation. Particularly when he glanced at Mrs. Galsworth and noted her heightened color.

James could not have said what devil it was in him that made him wish to upset the woman, but he could not deny the impulse was there. Between them, he and Miss Galsworth appeared to have done so quite thoroughly.

Not trusting himself, James rose and took his leave. He found himself accompanied by the entire group of gentlemen, who had already been there when he arrived.

He tried to demur. To be taking away with him Miss Galsworth's entire court was the outside of enough! But he could sway none of the gentlemen, and in the end, he had to give way with whatever good grace he could muster. On the street he discovered their purpose.

"Told Harrington you'd be by."

"Cotswold was the one pegged it for today."

"Why, Langford?"

Why? That was indeed the question. Why had he taken up her interest once and come again today to confirm it? James had no answer that satisfied himself, much less one that would satisfy these men.

So he shrugged, smiled his mysterious smile, and said, in a careless voice, "Why not?"

And with that he walked away, leaving the crowd of men arguing behind him.

He was weary, unaccountably weary. But he had no time for that. He had to send to the stables for his phaeton and pair. And change to clothes suitable to take a young lady out driving.

James paused for a moment, wondering just how old Miss Galsworth actually was. She did not seem a young chit, scarcely out of the schoolroom. Nor would he, despite an air of maturity about her, have guessed her to be much above twenty. But that left several years into which her age could fall.

Not that it mattered. How could it when he was only doing the polite? And yet James wondered.

If the Honorable James Langford was confused by his emotions, he was no more so than Miss Galsworth herself. On the surface, Mr. Langford was just the sort of simpleminded wastrel she could not abide. To be sure, he was kind, but kindness had never been sufficient to recommend a man to her before. Why should it do so now?

But it was not the kindness, Juliet thought as she ruthlessly tugged the comb through her curls, completely disarranging the style done so carefully for her earlier. And no amount of arguing could persuade her to don the gown her mother had said she ought to wear.

Instead, Juliet pulled a plain gown of dark green from her closet. She shook it out, noted the complete absence of bows and furbelows, and nodded in silent approval. For once she would dress to please herself.

Her maid stood by, aghast. "But miss! Your mother will be most unhappy with me. She was quite explicit. You were to wear the other green gown. The new one. The—"

"The one with all the white bows that make me look absurd," Juliet finished for her.

The maid giggled. "Well, yes, ma'am. It has perhaps a bit too much trimming. But your mother was most certain what she wanted."

"And I am equally certain of what I want. Come, help me into this gown. I shall delay until the last possible moment, going downstairs, and Mama will not have time to send me back upstairs to change. If she is angry, then I shall tell her it is all my fault—that I spilt something on the other and thought she meant I must wear green and this was the best I could do."

The maid shook her head but did as she was bid. Well before the time Mr. Langford was expected, Juliet was ready. She stood looking at her reflection in the mirror, her spectacles perched firmly on her nose. Gone were the curls that had been coaxed into creation with the help of a curling iron. Instead her cap of hair was combed far more becomingly around her face, though of course it would all be hidden by her bonnet anyway.

And the simple lines of her unadorned gown emphasized Juliet's height, instead of her breadth. She looked, she thought, almost acceptable.

Was it a mistake to wear this today? Before she had gotten to know Mr. Langford any better? When others might see her as well?

Impatiently, Juliet shook her head. It did not matter. She only knew she could not deny the impulse to do so. To show her true self to the man.

Which was absurd! He was an indolent dandy. No, not a dandy, they had established that already. Well, a wastrel then. Everyone said so. And yet, there had been a look of intelligence in his eyes that mirrored her own, both at the ball and earlier this afternoon. Something she had not expected to see. It was fanciful no doubt, but Juliet even found herself thinking that in Mr. Langford perhaps she had found a kindred spirit.

It was nonsense, all nonsense! No doubt he would tell her she looked much better with the curls in her hair and the bows and furbelows on her gown and she could dismiss him from her thoughts without further trouble.

But oh how she wished he would not.

Even as she stood there, caught up in her impractical, fanciful thoughts, someone rapped on the door and called out to her to hurry up, that Mr. Langford was already waiting downstairs.

Juliet and her maid looked at one another. Hastily she removed the spectacles that so offended her mother and tucked them into her reticule. She wished she dared wear them with Mr. Langford so that, for once, she would not need to squint and could see the city clearly. But even she knew that would be going too far.

The maid held out a bonnet and spencer to her mistress. Juliet took a deep breath and then took both, put them on, and went downstairs to meet Mr. Langford. Perhaps one day she could wear her spectacles in public, but not today.

Mama, of course, almost screamed at the sight of her daughter dressed so plainly. Nothing, Juliet thought, with a sense of despair, would ever convince the woman that her daughter did not look enchanting rigged out in all the nonsense she usually insisted upon.

Mr. Langford, when Juliet found the courage to meet his eyes, was staring at her as though stunned. He recovered quickly, however, as one would expect a gentleman to do. He bowed, offered her his arm, and headed for the doorway. Mama was still making inarticulate sounds behind them.

Outside, Mr. Langford handed her up into his phaeton with punctilious courtesy. Out of habit, Juliet glanced at the carriage itself, but it seemed in excellent condition. She nodded approvingly, which seemed to cause Mr. Langford to look somewhat taken aback and then amused.

"Do you approve of my equipage?" he asked, taking the reins from his helpful groom.

"It seems nice enough," Juliet conceded.

"I see. I would not ask," he said with a diffidence she suspected was not natural to him, "except that you seemed to be inspecting it with a particularly careful eye."

Juliet colored up, mortified. She dared not tell him the truth nor did she think she could successfully lie. Fortunately, the change in her appearance was sufficient to divert his thoughts.

"You look much better dressed like this," he said bluntly. "You ought always to dress in plain, simple lines."

"I wish you would tell that to Mama," Juliet retorted tartly. "She is convinced I must resemble some sort of doll or something and cannot resist ordering the most appalling decorations for my gowns."

He nodded. "I thought it might be her notion. But why do you allow it?"

Juliet gaped at him. Was he wanting in wits? She spoke slowly, as though convinced he was. "Mama pays the bills. Therefore, Mama has the power to make any modiste figure my dresses precisely as she wishes."

"How then do you come to have something as simple as this?" he asked, indicating her current attire.

Juliet's eyes narrowed, remembering. "I have this because I managed to slip it into my trunks when they were being packed. I wear it at home for gardening. Which Mama does not mind. Had she known I brought it to London, I've no doubt she would have taken a pair of shears to the fabric so that I could never wear it again. Which she may still do when I return home today," she acknowledged, a trifle sadly.

"No she won't," Mr. Langford said with great decision.

Juliet gaped at him again. It was becoming a habit. He seemed to notice for he smiled kindly at her and went on, "I shall make certain she doesn't. Indeed, I shall make certain she gives orders so that all the non-sense trimmings are removed from all your gowns."

That ought to have pleased Juliet but abruptly she found herself wishing for precisely the opposite. She found she did not want to have him cajole her mother in such a way.

"Oh, no! Pray don't!" Juliet objected quickly.

It was his turn to gape at her, a distraction to which his well-bred but high-strung horses took exception. He hastily got them back under control and then said, a speculative gleam in his eyes, "Now why would you not want me to do so?"

Juliet looked everywhere but at Mr. Langford. She waited for him to say something more. Instead he waited patiently. Finally, seeing no way out, she snapped, "If you must know, for all my complaints, I do not entirely disapprove. Indeed, I think of these absurd clothes that Mama makes me wear as a sort of test."

Chapter 4

A test? Was the girl mad?

"No, here now, Miss Galsworth! You cannot say such a thing and then not explain," James said, with pardonable exasperation.

But it seemed she felt she had already gone too far. And in any event, they were at Hookham's Lending Library. She looked surprised when he halted the carriage and tossed the reins to his groom, who had jumped down from behind.

"Well?" he said with the same note of exasperation as before, "I thought you wanted to find a book. You will find a great many here, you know."

Abruptly a smile lit up her face. "Yes, I did! And I thank you for being so kind as to bring me here. I didn't think you truly would."

She did not wait for him to hand her down, but managed the matter by herself. James frowned. Was she such a hoyden that she did not know how she looked, scrambling down in such a way? Or was she so caught up with the thought of books that she simply forgot?

He would have asked such a question about no other young lady he knew. But somehow it became important to know, in the case of Miss Galsworth, which might be true. Hastily he followed her into the shop.

Miss Galsworth went not to the shelves of novels, as he had expected, but to one tucked at the back with books of science. She seemed to know precisely which tome she was looking for. And they apparently did not have it, for her disappointment was patent.

James looked around and then coughed discreetly. "Er, if you told me what you were looking for, perhaps I could help. I have a rather extensive library of my own, you see," he added apologetically.

She looked at him doubtfully and he found himself bristling at the insult implicit in her air of disbelief. As a result, he so far forgot himself, and his pose as an indolent dandy, that he rattled off the authors and titles of several scientific texts he had in his study.

Her eyes widened in the most gratifying way and James added a few more titles. Now her lips parted with a tiny exclamation of awe and approval.

And when he clinched matters by stating that he had possession of the latest tome to be released, the precise tome she was looking for, Miss Galsworth clasped his hands with hers and said, admiringly, "My dear sir, I have clearly underestimated you!"

Just how far James would have forgotten himself, just how indiscreet he might have become, would fortunately never be known for at that precise moment a shrill female voice said, "James! How extraordinary to find you here. And at this time of day!"

James closed his eyes, then slowly opened them again. Miss Galsworth seemed to sense his distress for she hastily released his hands. He could feel her watching with great interest as he slowly turned and pasted a sickly smile upon his face.

"Athenia!" James said, with a marked lack of enthusiasm. "How are you? May I present Miss Galsworth? Miss Galsworth, my dear sister, Lady Darton."

The two ladies greeted one another warily. It would be hard to say which one gave the other the shrewder appraisal. Neither seemed enchanted by what she saw.

James all but shuddered as he recognized the too-sweet smile that now settled on Athenia's face.

"My dear Miss Galsworth. One has, of course, heard of you."

James wanted to step in front of the younger woman to protect her, but it seemed she neither wanted nor needed protection. In a voice just as sweet, just as false, as Athenia's she said, "And everyone, of course, has heard of Lady Darton."

Athenia all but preened. "I fancy I am rather well known," she agreed.

"Mr. Langford was just telling me how extensive a library he has," Miss Galsworth continued. "I am in awe of a family that values books so highly."

Athenia looked a bit more doubtful at this, but it was a compliment and so she regally inclined her head.

James held his breath, certain Miss Galsworth was about to say something outrageous. Instead she merely simpered, positively simpered, and said, "But oh dear, we must not take any more of your time, Lady Darton. I know how very busy you must be!"

And then while Athenia acknowledged this final compliment, Miss Galsworth sent him a silent plea and James hastily began to move toward the door.

"Miss Galsworth is absolutely right! Must go. Give my best to George."

And before Lady Darton could collect her wits sufficiently to recollect how she had meant to savage Miss Galsworth, they were out the door and he was handing her, with more haste than dignity, into the phaeton.

"That," he told her as they pulled neatly away from the curb, "was a narrow escape."

"Do you think so?" Miss Galsworth asked, with an assumed air of innocence. "Indeed, I found Lady Darton perfectly amiable."

"Yes, so long as you were feeding her compliments!" James retorted. "A fact of which I am somehow certain you were aware."

She did not deny it. Indeed, Miss Galsworth laughed. At his inquiring look she explained, "Lady Darton reminded me of Mama and, you see, I know what makes Mama happy."

James nodded. "Yes, well, I still say it was a fortunate escape." He paused then asked, "Shall I take you back home or would you like to drive around the park, after all?"

Miss Galsworth hesitated, then said, diffidently, "Would you mind greatly if we tried another lending library? I truly should like to find a copy of that book."

James threw all caution to the winds. "No need," he said recklessly, "I'll let you borrow my copy. I'll have it sent around or bring it myself tomorrow."

The smile on her face was sufficient to soothe whatever second thoughts James might have had. "Thank you!" she said, sounding almost breathless. "Then, yes, I should like to drive around the park."

They did so, having to stop constantly to greet friends of James's, for by now it was the fashionable hour to see and be seen. Still he managed to ask Miss Galsworth, "Why, by the by, do you wish to read that book?"

"Why, by the by, do you?" she countered.

He sputtered. "It is not at all the same thing," he protested. Then the obvious answer occurred to him, "Is it for a brother or perhaps your father that you were looking for the book? In that event, I could procure a copy for you directly from the publisher."

She looked at him with what James could only call contempt in her eyes. He was greatly taken aback. To be sure, there were times when he played his role as a rake a trifle too thoroughly and a young lady, or more likely her mama, had looked at him that way. But he had never been regarded with contempt over the question of a book!

In a cool, distant, polite voice Miss Galsworth said,

"On second thought perhaps I should write to the publisher myself to procure a copy. You need not trouble yourself further on the matter."

It wasn't sensible. He ought to simply agree and leave it at that. He and Miss Galsworth, after all, had nothing in common. But James found himself not being the slightest bit sensible.

Instead he looked at her and, with a grim edge to his voice, said, "Just what the devil is going on here, Miss Galsworth? If you were a man, I should believe that you and I shared the same interest in things mechanical. But since that patently cannot be the case, why the devil should you rip up at me over a book?"

James could see the effort she made to hold on to her temper. He could see the same battle waged in her eyes over what would be sensible. And he could see the moment she, just like he, lost.

"And why can that patently not be the case?" Miss Galsworth demanded hotly. "Just why can I not be interested in things mechanical? Because I am a woman?"

"Of course," James replied, surprised it even needed to be said.

Now she really lost her temper. Fascinated, James watched as Miss Galsworth looked around the park and then pointed to a nearby carriage. "There. That one is about to lose a wheel. And that one over there is not properly sprung. And—"

Before she could point to any more carriages and draw any further attention to the pair of them, James hastily said, "Yes, yes, that is quite enough. I believe you. You have an eye for carriages. But what has that to do with mechanical matters?"

"I also fix pumps. And I have initiated some changes in the way the laundry room is managed at my parents' estate, and I have a notion or two for the use of steam," she said, her voice perfectly even.

Behind him, James could hear the groom's instinctive recoil at such an unmaidenly confession. He ought, he supposed, to be shocked as well. And indeed he was taken by surprise. But Miss Galsworth's confession, or rather her listing of what she clearly considered her virtues, happened to tickle his fancy as well.

"Steam?" James murmured lightly. "In that event, perhaps we do have something in common, Miss Galsworth, after all," he said.

Now it was her turn to look at him with astonishment. And disbelief. "You? London's most indolent rake and wastrel? Nonsense! I will allow you may have read a book or two but that is scarcely the same as actually doing something with your knowledge."

That did it. All prudence, all thought of prudence, indeed all thought of any kind of propriety went straight out the window at her words. With a grim look in his eyes, James said, "Is that so, Miss Galsworth? Very well, I have something I wish to show you!"

And then, without any regard to common sense whatsoever, James proceeded to drive out of the park. Almost immediately he pulled the carriage to a halt, tossed a coin to his groom, and said, "Go home. I shan't be needing you any longer this afternoon."

The poor fellow tried to protest. To no avail. James was adamant. The groom looked to Miss Galsworth but she was not giving an inch, either.

"You'd best do as he says," she told the groom kindly.

Finally, shaking his head in strong disapproval, the fellow went. The moment he was walking away, James started the carriage up again and drove to a part of London that few members of the *ton* ever cared to visit. He drove to a large structure that was part of a factory and there handed the reins over to a workman standing idle.

Without a word, James handed Miss Galsworth down. She did not protest, did not threaten to faint or indulge in a fit of the vapors, did not even ask any questions. Instead she matched him, stride for stride, as he led the way to his workroom.

"No one knows about this," he said, unlocking the door. "At least no one in the *ton*."

Inside he pulled back the canvas that covered his pride, his joy, his obsession. He would have told her what it was, but there was no need.

She gave a gasp of pleasure and took a step forward. "An engine!" she said, in a tone of awe, running her gloved hand delicately over the metal.

James shoved his hands into his pockets and tried to look modest. He failed signally. In a gruff voice he said, "Runs on steam. I think it could power a carriage."

She looked at him, awe still in her eyes as she said, "Oh, yes, I should think so. Please, Mr. Langford, tell me everything about it!"

And he did. So apt a pupil was Miss Galsworth, that James soon found himself engaged in a discussion of the merits of various approaches to some of the problems he had yet to work out.

So apt a pupil was she that they both lost track of time. Her bonnet was soon abandoned on a chair, along with her gloves and spencer and his coat, gloves, and hat. She had long since retrieved her spectacles from her reticule and placed them securely on her face. An apron covered the front of her gown as another covered his shirt and trousers. Together they bent over the engine, examining every minute detail.

They talked about his other projects as well and James found that Miss Galsworth did not despise him for his inventions that went to factories.

"How did you come to take on such projects?" she asked with interest, not contempt in her eyes.

He wasn't going to answer her. He had never spoken of his reasons to anyone. Perhaps that was why he was so astonished to hear himself reply.

"I am not quite sure," he said. "I suppose it was

because of something I read in the papers. About how workers were being injured on a certain machine. And I thought that perhaps I could design something safer. Fortunately for me and for my pockets, mill owners were happy to buy it since not only was it safer but it would allow the workers to do their jobs better than before."

She looked at him then, really looked at him, and said, her voice full of emotion, "There are not many men who would have cared."

He was a fool to tell her more, but James could not help himself.

"My father would have cared," he said, his voice even more full of emotion than hers. "He was accounted a great reformer. If I have one regret, it is that I have not followed in his footsteps. I have not the courage. He was ostracized, you know, for his views. And we could not bear it, my brothers and I, as children. We did not understand. Even now I do not entirely understand it. I only know that there are times I think that if he could see the lot of us, he would only feel disappointment."

Her answer, when it came, startled James.

"Nonsense! Whatever good your father did, I'll wager you've done even more to help people by producing your inventions. And if you do not act openly, what is that to the point? You do a great deal more good than if you simply went about making useless speeches!"

It was a wonderment to James that Miss Galsworth patently meant every word she said. Nor did he doubt her sincerity when she added, "Do you have sketches of any of your inventions? For the mills, I mean? I should greatly like to see them. I have never before, you see," she said shyly, "met anyone who understood the things I like."

James found himself grinning. Miss Galsworth was the most unconventional young woman he had ever met and he found himself grateful for the hand of providence that had led to their unlikely acquaintance.

"I have a sheaf of sketches over here," he said, moving eagerly to the desk where he kept such things.

Together they bent over his drawings and Miss Galsworth seemed to have an inexhaustible supply of intelligent questions to ask him. Questions that James was delighted to try to answer, even when the young woman was able to point out little details he might have tried to improve his inventions even further.

Indeed, so engrossed were they that neither noticed when supper time came and went. Nor did either notice, beyond the need to light more candles, when it became dark outside. Neither noticed the hours pass until daylight began to peek in through the windows and the last of the candles began to burn out.

It was only then, when it was much too late, that they suddenly looked at one another, aghast, and said as one, "Oh Lord! Now we're in the suds!"

Chapter 5

Miss Galsworth was, if anything, the calmer of the two. "Perhaps, if we hurry," she said, pulling off her apron and reaching for a cloth with which to wipe her hands, "you can deliver me home and I can sneak in the back way without anyone being the wiser. I shall pretend I came home yesterday afternoon and went straight up to the attic and fell asleep there. I have done so before. Fallen asleep in the attic, I mean," she added hastily.

James snorted. "Do you really think they will believe such a Banbury tale?" he asked doubtfully.

"Have you any better notion?" she countered.

"No," he admitted slowly.

"Then don't you think it at least worth a try?"

James sighed, removed his own apron, and washed his hands in the nearby basin. "We must do something," he agreed. "I shudder to think what will happen if our families ever discover we were out all night together!"

Miss Galsworth did shudder. "It must not come to that," she said firmly. "And it shan't. Not if we hurry."

James was the first to realize just how mistaken she was. It occurred to him, as he guided his horses down the already crowded streets, that he could think of no way of letting Miss Galsworth down at her house without the pair of them being seen by someone's servants on the street. Still, he hoped that inspiration would come to him the closer they got.

Instead, as he turned onto the square he saw a carriage already standing in front of the Galsworths' town house. And, he realized with his own shudder, that it was his brother, Lord Darton, standing beside it.

It was too much to hope that George would not recognize James's turnout. Nor was there any way to retreat. Perhaps he could brazen it out and drive right past?

No, he didn't think so.

"James!" Lord Darton's voice rang out far too loudly in the quiet early morning air.

With a sigh of resignation, James drew his carriage to a halt behind Darton's.

"Who is he?" Miss Galsworth demanded with a hiss.

"My eldest brother, Lord Darton."

"What is he doing here?" she asked, patently bewildered.

"I don't know but it seems we are definitely in trouble now," James said, jumping down to greet his brother.

There was a look of thunder on George's face and it only darkened when he spied Miss Galsworth sitting in James's carriage. In a sharp but soft voice meant to reach only his brother's ears, Darton said, "I shall speak to the both of you, inside. We must do our best to keep the matter as quiet as possible."

Darton held a hasty whispered conversation with his groom and then the man, with a bit of maneuvering of the carriages, managed to arrange things so that he could hold the reins for both sets of horses.

As soon as that matter was settled, Lord Darton, James, and Miss Galsworth hastened up the steps.

"What the devil are you doing here? And at such an hour of the morning?" James demanded of his brother in a harsh whisper.

Lord Darton glared at his brother. "When you did not return yesterday with Miss Galsworth, her family, knowing me to be the head of our family, sent for me. I, naturally, reassured them that you must simply have been delayed but to send for me again this morning if you had not yet returned. It would seem they did not go to sleep at all, or rose remarkably early if they did, for the summons came this hour past. I shall not soon forgive you, James, for placing me in such an untenable position!"

There was no time to say more for they were already being shown into the Galsworth house and then led to the drawing room. They all three looked, James thought rather gloomily, like a party of prisoners on their way to execution. Which, considering the circumstances, perhaps they were.

Mrs. Galsworth and a man James presumed to be Mr. Galsworth were in the drawing room. The man was pacing while Mrs. Galsworth wrung her hands in dismay. At the sight of James and George and her daughter, the older woman gave a tiny cry of relief.

"What have you done to our Juliet?" the older man demanded in outrage.

"Juliet?" James echoed bewildered.

The girl beside him blushed. The older man and woman gaped. Even George looked at him as if he must have gone wanting in wits.

James looked at Miss Galsworth and said again, "Juliet?"

She nodded. The older couple sputtered. George frowned and asked in disbelief, "You spent the night with the girl and didn't even learn her name?"

Now it was James who blushed a fiery red. "We were, er, doing other things."

The gasps of outrage informed James that his reply had perhaps been infelicitous.

"That is to say, we were talking about other things!" he corrected himself with great haste.

But it was too late.

"He must marry her. He must!" Mrs. Galsworth said, weeping into a handkerchief.

"What the devil do you intend to do to make this right?" Mr. Galsworth demanded.

"Have you lost your wits entirely?" George asked, not troubling to hide his dismay.

James didn't even try to untangle the questions. He merely looked at Miss Galsworth, smiled wryly and half-apologetically to her, and then said, with a calm he was very far from feeling, "Miss Galsworth and I shall be married, of course. As soon as possible."

Abruptly silence descended over the room as if none of the occupants could credit that he had capitulated so swiftly. James looked at Miss Galsworth. Her eyes were wide and even she was staring at him in disbelief.

George mopped his brow and said, "I cannot say that I like it, but dash it all, under the circumstances I see no other alternative."

"Yes, yes, of course," Mr. Galsworth said, immediately expanding on this theme. "A notice must be sent to the papers at once."

"What I should like to know," Mrs. Galsworth broke in to say, in a firm but bewildered voice, "is what the two of you were doing all night?"

Again silence descended on the room as everyone gaped in disbelief at the woman. Her husband finally stammered, "What an absurd question! As if it matters. They were away, together, over night and must be married. And I don't care how many hearts you have broken," he told James sternly, "you will not break my daughter's."

"But was he seducing her?" Mrs. Galsworth asked, as if she could not quite credit such a thing.

James was a gentleman. Under ordinary circumstances a gentleman would never admit to having ruined a young lady. He would protect her by insisting they had just gotten lost, had a carriage wheel come off, or some other plausible story. But none of those would work in London.

"We were working on—" Miss Galsworth started to say.

Even as James realized she was about to tell the truth, he also realized that if she did so, it could only diminish her in the eyes of her family. Far better to let them think he had been carried away by passion. For it was patent that they all, George included, believed Miss Galsworth could not inspire such a thing.

So before she could finish her sentence, James pulled her into his arms, said loudly, "Yes, I was," and then kissed her quite, quite thoroughly.

There was only one little problem with this plan, aside from the fact that at first Miss Galsworth was struggling in his arms. James had very little practice kissing. Somehow, for all his reputation as a shameless rake, he had never really had a great deal of time for pursuing the ladies. How could he when machinery was his true passion? Not that he disliked the ladies, but even when he was presumed to be spending his time in brothels and such, James had actually been slipping out the back door and off to his factory workshop.

So now he had to concentrate and try to think of just how long he should hold the kiss, and where, precisely, he should place his hands, and just how fervent a kiss it should appear to be. But at least, he thought with some satisfaction, the trouble would be worth it.

He and Miss Galsworth had made a mistake, not taking note of the time. And now they would have to pay for it by getting married. Which would not, he thought, perhaps be such a horrible fate. It was true that he had not been dangling for a wife, but if he must marry, then Miss Galsworth at least possessed far more sense than any other young lady he had ever met. He might as well, for her sake, let everyone think he felt a grand passion for her. It would make things far more pleasant for the both of them.

By the time he let her go, James was more than halfway to regarding himself in the light of a protective, kindly, and even generous benefactor to poor Miss Galsworth. She, however, didn't seem to see things in quite the same way.

Juliet stared at Mr. Langford. His effrontery was beyond belief! Marry her? Without even asking her opinion of the notion?

To be sure, the look on Mama and Papa's faces and that of Lord Darton suggested they all thought he had no choice. But surely he couldn't believe such a thing? And yet, she had to admit she saw no other way out, either.

But why didn't he at least try to explain that they had merely been working on his invention? Well, if he would not, then she would tell them!

Juliet opened her mouth and started to speak and that was when he astonished her even further. He ruthlessly pulled her into his arms and began to kiss her!

Miss Galsworth struggled. She knew how improper such conduct was! How dare he handle her so? Particularly with Mama and Papa looking on?

And yet, without her quite knowing how it happened, Juliet ceased to struggle. Instead of pushing him away, her hands crept up to encircle his neck. And when his arms pulled her close against his body, she did not protest or pull away.

It was the most amazing thing that had ever happened to her, but Juliet found herself enjoying Mr. Langford's kiss. Was this why propriety forbade such things? Because it felt so . . . so delicious?

Juliet could think of no other word for the sensation. She felt a tingling all through herself and a strong desire for the kiss never to end. She liked, she discovered, Mr. Langford kissing her!

And then, as abruptly as he had pulled her to him, he let her go. At which point all of her sense and sensibility returned and Juliet turned a bright red, felt a flare of anger in her breast, and had to clench her fists to keep from slapping him.

He had such an air of smug self-satisfaction that she fairly itched to remove it from his face. How dare he? How dare he embarrass her in such a way before her family? And his brother?

Whatever would they think of her?

Just as Juliet opened her mouth to tell him how angry she was, her parents forestalled her. Was that approval she heard in their voices? It sounded suspiciously like approval, even if they were scolding Mr. Langford.

"Sir! That is most inappropriate behavior! I shall expect the notice to be sent to the papers at once and you are not to be alone with my daughter again before the wedding! Now about the settlements . . . "

"My Juliet! To be married!"

"Er, you had best let our solicitor speak with Mr. Galsworth's solicitor about the settlements, James. And I shall send the notice to the papers, if you like," Lord Darton hastily interjected.

"No, George, I shall send it," Mr. Langford said in a gentle but implacable voice. "As for settlements, why don't you and I go into your study, Mr. Galsworth, and decide them now?"

Juliet watched as Mr. Langford and her father retired from the room. With a curt bow in her direction, Lord Darton hesitated as though wondering whether he should follow, then took his leave. Feeling a trifle as though she had just been run down by a carriage, Juliet sank into the nearest chair. Her mother immediately sat beside her and took her daughter's hand in hers.

"Oh, my dear! Such an excellent marriage! That is to say, I am not entirely certain of Mr. Langford's prospects but he is the brother of Lord Darton and he has such a distinguished air about him! You will be the envy of all your friends! I never thought to see you captivate such a handsome man!"

"You mean, Mama, that you will be the envy of all your friends," Juliet said dryly. "And you never thought that would be the case. I know I have always been a disappointment to you."

Mrs. Galsworth avoided her daughter's eyes. "Not a disappointment, precisely," she said. "I will allow that I wish you had taken more interest in needlepoint and your music and less in things mechanical, but none of that is to the point anymore! You are to be married. And to the brother of Lord Darton."

She paused then said, with almost comic dismay, "I ought, of course, to scold you for spending the night with him. But as he is going to be a gentleman and marry you, I suppose it doesn't signify. So long as neither of you tells anyone, of course."

Juliet leaned forward. "Mama, the truth is that he was showing me one of his inventions and I was helping him work on it and we lost track of time," she said.

Now Mrs. Galsworth gave a shriek of dismay. "Don't ever say so!" she protested. "Far, far better, if the story of your disappearance overnight should be discovered, to let people believe you and Mr. Langford were indiscreet than to have anyone know how eccentric you are. How eccentric you both are! Oh, dear, I had no notion he wasn't a true gentleman. What your father is going to say, when he finds out, is beyond me."

Juliet sighed and put a hand over her mother's. "Papa is not going to find out because neither you nor I will tell him. Nor will Mr. Langford. It is all nonsense! I like Mr. Langford far better, now that I know he is not a hopeless fribble, than I did before."

Mrs. Galsworth clung to her daughter with pitiable desperation. "You do want to marry him, don't you, dear?" she asked.

"It cannot signify," Juliet retorted, with pardonable exasperation. "You and Papa and Lord Darton have all said we have no choice. To what point should I object? Mr. Langford and I shall simply have to make the best of it, regardless of what we feel."

Mrs. Galsworth could not help herself. She pulled her hand free and embraced her daughter. "You are so brave!" she exclaimed. Then, letting go of Juliet, she cleared her throat and her voice was once more the firm, somewhat martial tool it had always been. "We have no time to waste. There is a wedding to arrange. I wonder how soon it can be managed?"

Chapter 6

O ne might have thought matters could not get any worse. Juliet and James soon discovered they would have been mistaken in believing such a thing.

James was appalled to discover just how many of his friends thought it the most wonderful thing in the world that he had been caught in the parson's mousetrap.

"Not that anyone really thinks you a confirmed rake," Farnsworth explained, "but dash it all, you can't deny that you've been acting a trifle eccentric of late. It's a relief, you see, to find you taking so natural a step as marriage. At least that's what m'mother says."

"You're drunk," James told his friend bluntly.

"Am not! A trifle bosky, p'rhaps, but nothing more," Farnsworth protested indignantly.

"Maybe not," James said, "but you're talking instead of playing cards."

Most of Langford's other friends were more discreet but it was patent Farnsworth had spoken for the majority of them. The only blessing was that if any of them wondered at his choice of bride, none were rude enough to say so.

Except Sir Thomas Levenger. The same day that the notice appeared in the papers, James received a summons to appear before the venerable King's Counsel. For a summons it was, however politely couched as an invitation to dine at the home of Sir Thomas and Lady Levenger.

It ought not to have been an ordeal. Sir Thomas had stood godfather and then surrogate father to all the Langford brothers, George, Philip, James, and Harry. He had guided them gently for years, ever since the death of the late Lord Darton, James's father. And his wife, Lady Levenger, aunt to Philip's wife, was a quiet creature who could not frighten a flea. And yet James found himself shuddering as he stood on the bottom step in front of their town house.

Sir Thomas was the one person who might see through the deception. The one person who might guess what was behind it all. And what he would say was beyond James's ability to predict.

As always, the Levengers expressed delight to see him. Sir Thomas eyed him shrewdly, however, and even Lady Levenger was inclined to regard him with greater perception than was usual.

Still, they talked lightly of other matters during dinner and even after, when they were alone without the ears of servants to overhear. Sir Thomas began by asking about James's family.

"How is your brother Harry? Do you hear from him often?" Sir Thomas asked.

James frowned. "Not for some time. When last he wrote, he said there was some difficulty he was being asked to untangle. He didn't explain anything more and I knew better than to ask. But he did write to Philip, at about the same time, and tell him that the fighting is expected to be severe in the Peninsula and preparations were being made even as he penned his missive."

Lady Levenger sighed. "I do so wish your brother was safe at home!"

Now James smiled. "Do you, ma'am? Harry would not thank you for it! He says he is enjoying himself immensely. That he is needed."

"I've no doubt he is," Sir Thomas said thoughtfully. "Still, I should not be surprised to see him home soon. For a brief visit, that is."

"Why?" James asked.

There was a certain twinkle in the elder barrister's face as he replied, "Do you not recall? When your brother Philip became betrothed, Harry came home. Do you not think he will do the same for you?"

James shuddered at the thought. Harry would quiz him unmercifully! And remind him of the pact the three had made, he and Harry and Philip, never to marry. To be sure, Philip had been the first to break the pact; nonetheless, Harry would twit him for doing so as well.

Not that Harry had really come home because of Philip's betrothal. There had been other reasons, reasons unlikely to apply now. Still, he could say none of this aloud.

"I should be happy to see Harry, of course," James said, with a carelessness he did not feel, "but I think it most unlikely he would be granted leave for that."

Sir Thomas merely shrugged. "We shall see. But you must allow, the news of your betrothal is a most fascinating subject, for all and sundry, particularly those who know you well."

James, feeling a trifle desperate to turn the subject, said to Lady Levenger, "I've no doubt you've seen my brother Philip and his wife more recently than I. Has she undertaken any new crusades?"

Now a twinkle appeared in Lady Levenger's eyes and there was a note of innocence in her voice that deceived none of them. "Emily? Surely you have seen her latest article in the paper? About Bedlam? I should think there will be some changes there soon."

Sir Thomas snorted. "Don't believe it, Agatha! Nothing will change. They will tread lightly for a while, and perhaps even stop certain practices. But only for a little while. Then everything will be as before."

"You are a cynic, sir," James could not help but say.

"I am a realist," countered the barrister, a grim look about his eyes and mouth. "I wish it were otherwise. I have dedicated my career to making it otherwise. But I am a realist. Change will come slowly, if it comes at all."

"Then why do you still try?" James asked.

"Why did your father?" Sir Thomas countered. "He was far more of a firebrand than ever I could be."

Now an odd look appeared on James's face, a mixture of pride and pain. In even tones he said, "You know that my brothers and I have never understood our father. Or how he could cast away his good name on the sorts of crusades he undertook. It cost my mother, it cost all of us, dearly. If one cannot change things, why pay such a price for failing?"

"I did not say one cannot change things," Sir Thomas countered mildly. "I merely said that change comes slowly. And you must know I admired your father greatly. I have often wished I had his courage."

"Courage?" James echoed softly. "Perhaps, though George would say it was folly. He is forever pointing out that Father could not even drive his curricle at a sensible speed. That if he had, perhaps Father would still be alive today."

"Perhaps, perhaps not," Sir Thomas said, meeting James's eyes squarely. "Or perhaps there would simply have been another way for him to die."

"What the devil do you mean by that?"

"Yes, Thomas, what do you mean by that?" Lady Levenger echoed James with a puzzled note in her voice.

Sir Thomas hesitated, then shook his head. "It is not important. No doubt I am simply subject to the megrims whenever I think about your father. I have no reason to suppose anything untoward happened to him. At least not enough to give me the right to say so aloud. It is just that I thought him the last man in the world to be so careless. But come, let us talk of other things. How bad are your gambling debts?"

"Sir?" James asked, much taken aback.

"How bad are your gambling debts?" Sir Thomas repeated.

In a voice that was stiff with outrage, James replied, "I have none, sir."

"Perhaps I should ask: How bad were they before your betrothal?" the elder man countered.

Instantly James was on his feet. It took all his self-control to keep his voice even as he asked, "Is that what they are saying?" When Sir Thomas nodded, James said with the same outrage as before, "It is a calumny. I did not ask Miss Galsworth to marry me for her money."

"Well, why did you, then?" Lady Levenger demanded.

"And why the devil didn't you come to me, come to both of us, when you landed yourself in the briars?" Sir Thomas added impatiently.

"What makes you think I landed myself in the briars?" James demanded.

Sir Thomas gave him a derisive glance. "It will be much easier," he said, "if you sit down and simply tell us the truth of what occurred."

"We only wish to help," Lady Levenger added gently.

James sighed and sat. After a moment's contemplation, he told them everything. He told them about taking her to see his engine. He told them about showing her his sketches of the factory machines he had designed, and of her approval that he cared. He told them how it was dawn before either thought to take notice of the time.

When he was done, Sir Thomas shook his head. "Why the devil didn't you come to me?" he asked once again, this time with a wry gentleness. "Agatha and I might have helped you. If we said the pair of you were with us, no one could have caviled at it."

"I did not think of doing so," James answered candidly. "And in any event, it is too late to alter matters."

Sir Thomas was silent for a long moment. Then he looked at James and said, "Do you wish to marry the girl?"

James surprised even himself when he said, "Do you know, I think I do. Miss Galsworth is a sensible woman and shares my interest in things mechanical. And it has occurred to me that once I am married no one will be trying to foist their daughters on me anymore. Even George is likely to keep a less close eye on what I am doing."

Sir Thomas and Lady Levenger looked at one another, then she asked, cautiously, "But how do you feel about Miss Galsworth? Do you feel any affection for her?"

James blinked. "What has that to say to the matter? We must be married and we are both sensible people. We shall manage tolerably well and what more can one ask?"

Again the older two looked at one another and this time they both blushed. With a certain gruffness in his voice Sir Thomas replied, "There can be, er, a great deal more. Perhaps one day you and Miss Galsworth will discover something of that sort as well. Meanwhile, if we can be of any service to the pair of you, please let us know."

"I shall," James said, and he did not need to feign the gratitude he felt.

Juliet was having no easier a time of it. She suddenly found herself to be the most interesting young lady in London. Or so it seemed from the steady stream of callers who now flocked to the Galsworths'

town house. And from the number of gentlemen who
solicited her hand for dancing or the number of ladies
who suddenly recollected that they had forgotten to
send her invitations to some social event.

It had not taken long for Juliet to realize that everyone wanted to know how she, such a plain girl, had
managed to captivate one of London's most elusive
bachelors! And she, frustrating as it was, could not
tell them. Not even though she knew some were wondering aloud just how large a dowry her father had
settled on her and whether it had been gambling debts
that forced Mr. Langford to offer for her.

It would not have been so bad if she and James
could have had time alone. If they could have had the
chance to talk about this marriage. Or even, and Juliet
blushed at her own thoughts, if they could have been
alone so that Mr. Langford could repeat his kiss.

It might have helped if they could have worked on
his engine again. Or even just talked about that or his
other projects. Somehow knowing that her betrothed
cared enough about workers to try to design machines
that would be safer for them warmed her heart. Whatever the world thought, she knew he was not a useless
dandy and wastrel. If only she could have told him so,
if only he could have reminded her of all the reasons
she had found him such an enjoyable companion on
that momentous night.

But it was not to be. Mr. Galsworth was as good as
his word. He made certain there was no possibility of
even the slightest tête-à-tête between his daughter and
Mr. Langford. They were the focus of all eyes during
any encounter whatsoever and interested ears hovered
to hear what captivating conversation might ensue.
For no one, it seemed, could believe Miss Galsworth
had drawn Mr. Langford's interest with her looks.

Juliet's greatest trial, however, was Lady Darton.
She came to call at an unusually early hour one day
and explained herself by saying, "I know you will for-

give me. I wished to be certain to have a chance to speak with Miss Galsworth without the whole world present to overhear."

"Naturally," Mrs. Galsworth said.

Juliet eyed Lady Darton warily. Indeed, she found herself so overawed by the woman that she could think of nothing to say.

"Lord Darton has told me, of course, of the circumstances of this betrothal between Miss Galsworth and Mr. Langford," Lady Darton continued austerely. "I cannot say that I approve of what took place; however, I do concede the necessity that matters be remedied as quickly as possible. And I should never suggest that Mr. Langford shirk his duty."

She did not mention their encounter at the lending library, a small mercy for which Juliet was grateful. Still, she could not think of a word to say in reply other than to murmur, "You are very kind."

Lady Darton permitted herself a small, thin smile. "I try to be," she agreed. "That is why I am here. To assure you that once you and Mr. Langford are wed, I shall make it my responsibility to show you how to go on, for it is clear you lack town bronze."

Her ladyship then turned to Mrs. Galsworth and spoke with her for a short while concerning details of the wedding itself. Finally she rose to her feet.

"I have stayed long enough, I am expected elsewhere. I am pleased to see that you are not a chatterbox, Miss Galsworth. While I cannot approve of the conduct which brought you to this pass, I shall concede that matters could have been much worse. Much worse indeed."

Mrs. Galsworth accompanied Lady Darton to the front door, fluttering about her and thanking her for her condescension in coming to call.

Juliet, however, stayed behind and paced the small drawing room. Lady Darton condescended to be satis-

fied? She conceded that matters could be much worse?
It was difficult, in Juliet's opinion, to see how.

And she could not help but wonder if the entire
Langford family—except James, of course—was this
dreadfully starched up. To be sure, she had heard odd
rumors about the brother who was a barrister and his
wife, but she paid them little mind, knowing how false
such things could be.

No, the odds were the entire Langford family was
starched up and she would be found even more wanting than she was by her own family. Why had she ever
agreed to this match? If only she could cry off!

A tiny corner of her heart, however, suggested that
it would be equally acceptable if the ceremony were
simply over and done with. At least then she and Mr.
Langford would be allowed to be alone together.

Chapter 7

The night before his wedding, James found himself in his rooms surrounded by all three of his brothers, George, Philip, and even Harry home on leave. This quite naturally prompted Sir Thomas, who was there as well, to remind James that he had predicted Major Langford would return in time for the wedding.

Several bottles of wine had been opened and the conversation was lively. It was perhaps no surprise that by midnight the advice was flowing freely.

"You must treat her with the greatest respect," George said pontifically. "Women do not feel as we do about, er, physical needs."

Sir Thomas gave a snort of disbelief but refused to elaborate. It was Philip who said quietly, "You must understand that women are different creatures than we are. They look at matters rather differently and must be handled carefully. They must be humored."

Sir Thomas quirked an eyebrow upward but still refused to speak. James turned to Harry.

"Have you any advice for me?" he asked, not troubling to hide the sarcasm in his voice.

Harry shrugged. "I should have advised you not to get entangled, but since you are, I defer to the greater wisdom of those who have trod the path before you."

James took another deep drink of his wine then turned to Sir Thomas. "What, sir, do you advise?"

The barrister hesitated. Then he smiled. "Talk to your wife. Listen to what she has to say. Do not dismiss it out of hand simply because it is a different perspective than you would have chosen."

"That shall be no hardship," James replied with a secretive smile that greatly intrigued his brothers, though none quite dared to ask him what it meant. "Miss Galsworth has a mind that is exceptional. And fortunately she will understand my interests because she shares them."

"Well of course she does," George said, puzzled that James thought such a thing needed to be stated. "It is her duty to do so."

Both Philip and Sir Thomas managed, though not entirely successfully, to smother guffaws. George looked affronted. "James," he continued, defensively, "begin as you mean to go on. You must not allow Miss Galsworth to attempt to rule the roost or you shall regret it."

"Is that what Athenia did?" Harry asked, his expression all innocence.

"Don't be a fool!" George retorted.

With patent effort, Philip and Sir Thomas refrained from baiting George any further. For several moments there was silence and then James blurted out one of his fears.

"How do I make her happy?" he asked.

George gaped at him. Harry smothered laughter of his own. Sir Thomas, however, nodded approvingly and Philip gave him a curious smile.

When none of them answered him, James persisted. "How do I make my wife happy? Surely it is not such a difficult answer as all that."

Harry cleared his throat. "If you mean how do you satisfy a woman in bed—?"

"Good God!" George exclaimed. "James is talking about his wife, not some street strumpet! Your bride," he told his younger brother earnestly, "will not expect anything of the sort from you. She will do her duty and that is all either of you need worry about there."

"That isn't what I meant," James said hastily. "But I do think it a shame if she cannot be happy in bed as well as out of bed."

George turned a bright red.

In a careless tone Sir Thomas said, "Darton thinks that because Miss Galsworth is a lady she will be above such things. He may or may not be correct."

"Indeed, he could be quite incorrect," Philip chimed in, a look of patently false innocence upon his face.

James closed his eyes, then opened them. "Never mind the bedroom," he said hastily. "No doubt Miss Galsworth and I shall manage that part. What about in other ways? How am I to make my wife happy?"

"Give her a generous allowance and a few extra fripperies from time to time?" George suggested.

Sir Thomas kept his face impassive, though his lips twitched once or twice as he replied, "I believe I already answered that question when I told you to listen to your bride. Ask Miss Galsworth what she wishes. No doubt she will tell you and all you need do is listen to know what will make her happy."

Philip rubbed the side of his nose. "It may not be quite that simple," he cautioned, "but it is an excellent place to start."

Harry, who had been listening thoughtfully, now said, "The question is, will Miss Galsworth be able to make you happy, James?"

James stared down into his glass. His head buzzed with the oddest sensation and he found himself wondering just how much he had had to drink. Certainly several bottles lay empty on the table. In the end he decided it didn't matter, for even had he been completely sober, his answer would have been the same.

He smiled at his brothers and there was a far-off gleam in his eyes. James could scarcely tell them about the night he and Juliet had spent together, working on his steam engine. Nor the fact that she was the only person he had ever told about why he began inventing mill machinery.

And yet, though he could tell his brothers none of that, James did say, softly, "Do you know, Harry, I rather think she will."

At her home, Juliet was also receiving advice. Hers came from her mother. "You are not to show any interest in his outside interests."

"But Mama, he likes that I took an interest in his engine."

Mrs. Galsworth colored up. "I am not talking about engines!" she declared.

"But Mama," Juliet persisted, more confused than ever, "what do you mean? Do you mean his other scientific interests? Or if he should be interested in art or music or some such thing?"

"No, that is not what I mean!" Mrs. Galsworth said, driven by exasperation to speak bluntly. "I am talking about women. Other women."

"But is he not to have friends?" Juliet asked.

"Of course he will have female friends," Mrs. Galsworth said carefully, still trying to handle things in a delicate manner. "It is just that they will not be females you ought ever to acknowledge much less tax him with."

"But why can they not be my friends as well?"

"Do not be deliberately obtuse," Mrs. Galsworth snapped. "I am not talking about women of our class! I am talking about opera dancers or light skirts or other disreputable creatures. You are to pretend they do not even exist, much less speak of them to Mr. Langford."

Juliet twisted her hands together. A thousand daughters must have been given just such a talk on the night before their wedding, she thought. Why should it hurt so when it was her turn? But it did.

"Is he not to notice my male friends, then?" Juliet asked, determined to pretend there was nothing extraordinary about anything her mother was saying.

Now Mrs. Galsworth shrieked, positively shrieked. "You are not to have male friends," she said. "Certainly not before you have given Mr. Langford an heir. Preferably two sons. And best not ever."

Was that so? A tiny tear trickled down Juliet's cheek. Her mother pretended not to notice.

"It does not seem fair," Juliet said in a small voice.

"Well, what an absurd notion!" her mother exclaimed. "Of course it is not fair. What has that to say to anything? It is the truth. That ought to be enough for you. Do you not pretend to be an intelligent, a scandalously intelligent, young woman? Well, then, I ought not to have to explain things any further. They ought to be self-evident to you."

"Yes, Mama," Juliet said, with a tiny sniff.

But she was not and had never been, much to her mother's regret, a fainthearted creature. So now Juliet drew in a deep breath and then said, in a much firmer voice, "I shall simply have to make certain Mr. Langford has no desire to . . . to seek the company of other females."

"Juliet!" Mrs. Galsworth said in a scandalized voice that held a hint of fear. "Whatever do you mean?"

She met her mother's gaze steadily as she took another breath and said, "I mean that I must do whatever it is these other females do to attract men."

Mrs. Galsworth felt a strong desire to faint. She knew, however, her duty, and she would not shirk it. "You are not ever to speak in such a way again!" she said. "The notion that you, a lady, should compete with . . . with Covent Garden wares! Why, if anyone should overhear you say such a thing, it would be the ruin of you, marriage or not! You must not say such a thing ever again. No, nor think it either."

"But might not Mr. Langford like the notion?" Juliet asked hesitantly.

Mrs. Galsworth shook her head, dismay patent in her expression. "No! Indeed not, my dear! You cannot understand, of course, but a man wants a lady in his wife, not a wanton creature. If you tried to imitate them, you would only succeed in giving him a disgust of you! Promise me you will put the notion out of your mind. At once!" she commanded.

Juliet looked at her hands. They seemed such large, ungainly things. How could Mr. Langford wish to marry her? Nervously she twisted her hands together in her lap, and sighed yet once again. Was her mother right? She supposed she must be for she had, after all, so many years of experience. It was a most lowering thought.

"Well, Juliet? Did you hear me?" Mrs. Galsworth demanded.

"Yes, Mama," she answered meekly.

Mrs. Galsworth did not trust this acquiescence, but what was she to do? In the morning Juliet was to be married to Mr. Langford. Well, then it would be his problem and not hers. She thanked God for that simple favor. And after all, this marriage was much better than any she had thought to expect for Juliet. No, instead of worrying, she ought to be grateful that anyone, much less the brother of Lord Darton, had chosen her clumsy, ungainly, most unfeminine daughter.

Before she could betray her thoughts, Mrs. Galsworth hastily rose to her feet and said, "You should go to sleep now, Juliet. Tomorrow you are to be married and you will wish to look your best."

Then, with a proud glance at the wedding dress that hung by the looking glass, ready for morning, Mrs. Galsworth took her candle and left her daughter's room.

Once she was gone, Juliet's gaze strayed to precisely the same point as had her mother's. It strayed to the gown covered with bows and little fabric nosegays and ruffles all around the neck and sleeve and hem. And a glint came into her eyes that would have greatly alarmed Mrs. Galsworth had she been present to see it.

"I may have to be married in the morning," she muttered, "but I shall go as myself, not the ridiculous creature Mama has always tried to pretend I must be. And if Mr. Langford does not like it, well, he can cry off."

With a grim determination that her parents knew all too well, Juliet moved toward the gown. She circled it twice, fingered the fabric a time or two, tugged experimentally at one of the bows, and then set to work in earnest. For once her sewing scissors were being turned to a purpose that Juliet could accept.

It was late when Juliet was at last satisfied. Her mother would hate what she had done, but Juliet would feel herself when she walked into the church on the morrow.

Carefully she blew out the candles in her room and climbed into bed. She did not expect to be able to sleep, but somehow, with the dress altered to be more what she wished, Juliet felt at peace. And she was dreaming long before anyone would have guessed it would be possible for her to do so.

Chapter 8

James rose, his head aching. His gaze fell on the remains of the previous evening's celebration. His valet stood by, a long-suffering expression on his face.

"What is it, Woods?" James asked with a resigned sigh.

"You ought to have risen an hour ago," the valet replied. "As it is, I calculate you shall barely have time to dress and eat before it is time for you to depart for the ceremony. Nor have you deigned to tell me where you intend to spend your wedding night or how long you will be gone on your wedding journey. I cannot pack for you until you do so."

"Wedding night?" James echoed, a sinking sensation in the pit of his stomach. "Journey?"

The valet looked at a point above his employer's head. "No doubt I have somehow fallen into your bad graces that you chose not to tell me. But the time is growing short, and if you are to be ready to leave on your wedding journey today, I must know how to pack for you. And whether you intend that I should accompany you. But perhaps you have already decided to replace me?"

"Replace you? I should think not!" James retorted in dismay. "No, by God, Woods, I simply forgot about a wedding journey. I've made no plans! What the devil am I to do now? And why didn't anyone remind me before this?"

This last was muttered to himself and the valet was too shrewd to attempt to answer such an unanswerable question. Instead he unbent sufficiently to cough and suggest, "Perhaps, sir, I could make a reservation for you at a suitable establishment here in London and then you could decide where you wish to go after that."

James felt as though his head were unpardonably thick this morning. "Why not simply bring her back here for tonight?" he asked.

It was Woods's turn to gape. "It is your wedding night, sir!"

"Miss Galsworth won't mind," James said, beginning to move about the room. "She's a sensible gel."

"She may be a sensible young lady," Woods countered, "but I should lay odds that her family would take it as a great insult if you did not treat her in a more respectful manner than to bring her back to your bachelor quarters on her wedding day."

James sank onto the bed and held his aching head in his hands. "You are right, of course," he said mournfully. "Very well, make whatever arrangements you think best. Just tell me what else I have forgotten to do."

Woods regarded the ceiling with great interest. He coughed. "Have you, er, made any arrangements, sir, as to the establishment in which you and Mrs. Langford will reside after your, er, honeymoon? And have you hired a staff for whatever house you may have chosen?"

James glanced around. He did not even try, this time, to suggest that his current set of rooms would do. Instead he groaned.

"I have done none of that, curse you," he growled to Woods. "Why did you say nothing of this before today? It's a trifle late, don't you think?"

The valet merely raised his eyebrows in surprise. "It was not my place to say so, sir. It would be for your friends or family to speak, if they thought it necessary."

The man was right, of course, and that only made James curse again. "I suppose I shall have to either ask you to find something or," he added hastily at the look of disdain on his valet's face, "rather perhaps my man of business. He can look into the matter for me. I suppose I'd best write him to that effect before I even try to get dressed. There is no time to be lost!"

Woods merely bowed, his face impassive. James was not deceived. He had managed to fall dismally short of his valet's expectations, and that did not set well on the morning of his wedding. It did not seem, he thought gloomily, a particularly auspicious beginning.

Later, as James hastily dressed for his wedding, he realized that any number of people around him, including his brother George, had tried to hint to him the need to address the matter of lodgings and servants and honeymoons and such. But he had not paid attention.

He could only hope that Woods could at least manage something suitable for tonight. But then, that was why he paid his valet twice the amount any other valet in London was paid. Because the man recollected all the things James was so prone to forget and he could manage at the last moment to retrieve matters when necessary.

Meanwhile, he was about to be married and it occurred to him that his bride, Miss Galsworth, might be feeling a trifle nervous as well. If so, it would be his duty to put her at ease.

Juliet was woken by the sound of her maid shrieking. Bleary, she opened her eyes and said, frowning, "What's wrong, Margaret?"

"Your wedding gown, miss! Someone's destroyed it!"

That brought Juliet fully awake. She swung her feet over the edge of the bed and stood up. She moved hastily to lock the door in case anyone came to see why the maid had shrieked. Juliet was not quite ready to face her family yet. It was bad enough to have to tell her maid, Margaret, the truth.

"I did it," Juliet said quietly.

The maid looked at her with very wide eyes. Almost as though she thought her mistress had gone mad. And perhaps she had, Juliet mused silently.

Aloud she said, "I could not bear to wear it with all the fabric flowers and bows and ruffles, Margaret. Please don't tell my mother. Let her see when it is too late for her to attempt to put them back on."

The maid hesitated. "Mrs. Galsworth will blame me," she said cautiously.

"I shall take the blame," Juliet said firmly, "but I shall not go to my wedding dressed as though I were some dressmaker's doll! Mr. Langford must take me as I am and I am plain, not the dainty creature Mama has always wanted for a daughter and I presume that he wanted for a wife."

"Oh, no, miss! He couldn't want a better bride than you!" Margaret replied.

Juliet smiled at her maid. "I thank you for that. Will you keep quiet about the gown?"

The maid looked one more time at the dress surrounded by fluffs of fabric and trim all over the floor and nodded. "It will cost me my position, I've no doubt, but I will."

"It won't cost you anything," Juliet said firmly, "for you shall come with me after the wedding. I shall need a maid and why not you?"

That silenced the last of the maid's qualms, and Juliet felt a pang of guilt that she had not reassured the girl sooner as to her future. But it had never occurred to her that Margaret might think she would not be welcome in Juliet's new household.

There was a great deal, she thought with a sigh, to being mistress of a household. Engines and all things mechanical she understood only too well. Servants and kitchens and housekeeping were another matter entirely.

A rap at the door drew her out of her reverie and both she and Margaret started. They looked at one another with a sense of panic. Could it be Mama? It was.

"Juliet? Are you awake? May I come in?"

"No! Not yet, Mama! Later. I wish to be alone for a while," Juliet called out.

"Very well. I shall give you an hour. And then you had best be dressed for it would not do to be late to the church," Mrs. Galsworth called out.

Both Margaret and Juliet looked at one another as they heard the older woman walk away, relief patent on both their faces.

"Well," Juliet said, taking a deep breath, "I guess I'd best get ready for my wedding day. Once I am in the dress, Mama will not be able to do anything about it. And Margaret," she added thoughtfully, "I think we will dress my hair plainly, without the curls today."

Now the maid took a deep breath. "Yes, miss," she said. "Just as you wish. And," she added with a rush of bravado, "I shan't care a rush for anything your mama says to me afterwards!"

"Bless you, Margaret!"

If she was not ready in quite an hour, Juliet took no more than twenty minutes more than that. And when she looked in the mirror, in the end, it was worth everything she had done, all the anger she risked. Because for once the woman who looked out at her from her mirror was Juliet, not some creature tricked out in clothes chosen by her mother.

"Miss, your mother's pounding something fierce. Should I open the door?" the maid asked.

It was only then that Juliet became aware of the sound she was hearing. Margaret was quite right. By now the pounding was urgent on her bedroom door. Juliet bravely put her spectacles on and signaled to Margaret to let her mother into the room.

"Juliet!"

Mrs. Galsworth snatched the spectacles from Juliet's face. Only a moment later did the enormity of what had been done to the wedding dress impress itself on Mrs. Galsworth's awareness. Her anguished cry could no doubt be heard throughout the entire house.

Juliet pretended she did not understand. "But I wish to wear my spectacles so that I can see my husband clearly," she said in a reasonable voice.

"I do not give a fig about your spectacles!" her mother snapped. "You shall not wear them, and do try not to squint. But it is your dress I am concerned about! How could this have happened?"

Juliet allowed her mother to vent all her spleen. Only when the woman had run out of things to say did she speak.

"Mama, I know you are distressed, but we have no time to alter matters. We are expected at the church."

There could be no answer to that except for Mrs. Galsworth to continue to scold all the way there.

"I do not know what Mr. Langford will say when he sees you. He will think we have cheated him. I wash my hands of you, Juliet!"

There was a great deal more in this vein but Juliet chose not to listen. Useless to point out to Mama that Mr. Langford had liked her far better in the plain dress the day he took her out for a drive. For to point that out would be to remind both her parents of the scandalous behavior that had caused this precipitous marriage in the first place.

Besides, from the moment of her birth and no doubt before, Mama had believed that only a dainty creature swathed in ruffles and ribbons and bows could ever be considered truly feminine. That was not likely to change now, no matter what Juliet said.

Timidly Mr. Galsworth tried to come to her defense. "I do think Juliet looks quite nice," he said.

"You know nothing of it!" Mrs. Galsworth exclaimed in exasperation.

"Papa is a man," Juliet could not resist pointing out.

It did not help. "It is just that sort of distasteful levity which is likely to cause you trouble," her mother warned.

Juliet and Mr. Galsworth exchanged glances but neither said another word. Not until they reached the church. And not even then except that Papa did lean toward her and say, "I do hope you will be happy, my dear. This is not how I should have liked it all to happen, but now that it has, I hope you will learn somehow to make the best of it."

Juliet could not answer. How to say that a tiny corner of her heart did not mind being married today? That a tiny corner of her heart already looked forward to being with Mr. Langford every day? Even, she thought with a blush, to having him hold her in his arms again and kiss her. For he surely would have to do so, once they were married. Wouldn't he?

But there was no more time for such reflections. It was time for the ceremony to begin.

Chapter 9

It could not be denied that Mr. and Mrs. Galsworth felt a great sense of relief once the knot was safely tied. They were effusive as they directed everyone present to come back to their town house for the wedding breakfast.

Lord and Lady Darton were noticeably less pleased. To be sure, Lady Darton was condescendingly kind to Juliet and Lord Darton said all that was proper but their expressions made it evident to all that this was not how they would have chosen to arrange matters.

Philip and Emily Langford, by contrast, were all that was kind to Juliet. And Harry joked that his brothers seemed to be discovering the finest ladies in England and that by the time he returned for good, after the war was over, there would be none left for him.

In spite of her nervousness, Juliet could not resist laughing at his good-natured jesting.

But it was Sir Thomas and Lady Levenger who most made her feel welcome to the Langford family.

"I confess, that when I first heard that James was to be married, I was a trifle concerned. He has been like a son to me, you know," Sir Thomas told her, a twinkle in his eyes. "But once I saw you, I knew that you would do. I have long hoped he would find someone precisely like you to make his life complete. Now that he has, I am very pleased to be able to wish you happy."

Lady Levenger was even more effusive. "My dear, I wish you every happiness! You and James will deal extremely well together and I cannot help but think him very fortunate to have found you!"

All might have been well had that been the end of it. But of course it was not. Lady Darton managed to draw Juliet aside and attempt to engage her in conversation.

"Do you and James mean to live in London?" she asked.

Juliet hesitated. Her smile faltered a trifle. "I am not entirely certain," she said. "That is to say, he has not told me what he plans. But I should like," she said with a little more certainty, "to live in London."

Lady Darton permitted herself to smile kindly. "So you do not wish to draw James away from his interests here? You like the city?"

Here at last was a question she could answer without fear! Juliet smiled, her happiness apparent to anyone watching. "Indeed I do, Lady Darton. I have been amazed and delighted at all the marvelous exhibits to be found in this city. And I should dearly like to attend some scientific salons. I trust James will be willing to take me."

On and on she went, oblivious to the way Lady Darton increasingly stiffened in disapproval. It was not until James realized what was happening and, coming close enough to overhear, slid an arm around her waist and pinched her in warning, that Juliet realized her words were not meeting with approval. She broke off with a stammered, "Oh, dear!"

"Oh, dear, indeed," Lady Darton sniffed. "You do not seem to comprehend that your first duty as James's wife is to present him with an heir and to preside over any social functions he wishes to hold. I do not disdain learning in a woman," she said with a thin smile. "Indeed, I should find it deplorable if you did not have a suitable degree of knowledge. But it is one thing to be educated and quite another to set oneself up as a veritable bluestocking! That is something I cannot and will not permit. There are females who do so, of course, but I cannot call them ladies."

Juliet was so stunned by this attack that she could think of nothing to say. James, however, was not. In his gentle, well-bred voice he said, "But it is not for *you* to choose, Athenia, what *my* bride will or will not do. She is and will always be a lady. Nothing you or others might say could ever change that simple fact."

Lady Darton visibly gathered her dignity to her. She ignored the last part of his statement. Instead she drew in a deep breath and said, "Yes, of course. It is indeed for you to say. I do trust you will teach your wife how to properly conduct herself. After all, no one has ever caviled at your manners or behavior."

Juliet bristled. She could not help herself. She wanted to say that it was her life and that it was for her to decide what was appropriate for her. But she knew only too well with what derision and disapproval Lady Darton and her own parents and perhaps even James would greet such a notion. So she kept silent and brooded. It was, after all, only one more reminder of the change in her estate and there was no point in denying it.

Or rather, Juliet would have kept silent had Lady Darton not nodded approvingly and added, "I will allow, James, that at least your bride can hold her tongue."

"I wish, Lady Darton," Juliet said in the quiet voice that always roused her parents' worst fears, "you would not speak as if I was not here. Or as if you thought I was deaf. I am capable of speech and thought and even independence of action. Just as you are so evidently capable of acting and speaking independently of your husband!"

By the time Juliet was done, bright spots of red marred Lady Darton's cheeks. She visibly bristled. Most of those who had gathered close to listen to the conversation now visibly drew back from the outrage they patently expected Athenia to unleash upon Juliet.

All, that is, save Lord Darton. He chuckled and moved closer. Indeed, he moved close enough so that he could put his arm about his wife's waist, ignoring her efforts to evade him. He then dropped a kiss on the top of her head, causing Athenia to bristle even more.

But then Lord Darton's voice came soft and low and affectionate as he said, "I recall another bride who spoke sharply on her wedding day, my love. A bride it took all my efforts to gentle. But a bride I would not trade for any other. Or for any price in the world!"

To the astonishment of everyone in the room, save perhaps Lord Darton, the lines of Lady Darton's face softened and she leaned toward him. Her voice held a softness, a gentleness none of them had ever heard before when she replied.

"Truly, George?"

Lord Darton beamed down at his wife. "Truly, my beloved," he assured her in a voice full of tenderness.

As one they moved away, leaving the others in the room to gape at one another in astonishment. Major Harry Langford was the first to recover his wits. A smile lit his face with unholy glee.

"Beloved! He called her his beloved!"

Philip, on the other hand, sounded almost gently pleased as he said, "So he did. Perhaps we have misjudged George and his marriage after all."

It was left to Sir Thomas Levenger to break the spell of astonishment they all seemed to be under. "Young puppies, the lot of you!" he said to the Langford brothers. He paused to stare down at Lady Levenger and pat her hand affectionately. "When you are

my age, you will know how rare true love is and how
well it ought to be cherished, no matter in what
strange guise it may appear."

That was enough to break up the cluster and they
all moved to mingle with the other guests. Something
for which Juliet's parents were profoundly grateful.
They had not wished to intrude, but the interchange
had drawn far too much attention. Really, there were
moments when the Langford clan seemed quite eccentric! The Galsworths did not like eccentricity, not in
any form. Particularly not when it in any way touched
their daughter.

Perhaps, Juliet thought, she was more like her parents than she had supposed for she found the encounter with the Langfords most unsettling. Still she took
comfort in having James by her side. And it was almost as if he knew how she felt for he made no move
to leave her.

Juliet could not later recollect what was served or
if she even tasted any of the food. All of her attention
was on the man beside her, who seemed as if he did
this sort of thing every day. For him there seemed to
be no terrors, no second thoughts, no reservations.

He laughed and jested with his family, and with
hers, as though there were nothing out of the ordinary
about their union. How she wished it were so! Was
he thinking of tonight, as she was? Of their days
ahead together?

And when he looked at her and smiled, Juliet felt
as if all her fears were melting away. It was absurd,
for how could a smile do such a thing? And yet it did.
When he reached out his hand to her, she put hers in
his and knew that with this man she was safe. That
whatever lay ahead, they would forge their new life
together.

Nor did James look at her as if she were a disappointment to him, as Mama always did. He looked at
her, impossible as it seemed, as if she were just the

woman he wanted to see at his side. She would have loved him for that alone and she clung to him, grateful for the way he made her feel.

But there did come a moment when circumstances separated them and it was then that she found a woman of medium height, with pretty blonde hair and blue eyes, beside her. The woman smiled in a friendly, open fashion that Juliet could not help but like.

"Hello. I am Philip's wife."

"Are you truly a reformer?"

The words were out before Juliet had time to consider whether she ought to say them and there was no way to call them back. But Emily did not seem to take offense. Instead she smiled warmly, glanced about, then pressed Juliet's hand with her own.

In a low voice meant not to carry to other ears, Emily Langford said, "If you know that much about me, then you know we shall be friends. I only wished to let you know that Philip and I shall do everything we can to ease your way within the family."

And then, before Juliet could think of what to say to these kind sentiments, the other woman moved away. It was both a reassuring and an unnerving encounter and Juliet could not say which was the stronger emotion.

Her own relatives crowded around, patently eager to know how their oddly inclined Juliet had managed to ensnare such a dandified wastrel. It was not, after all, as though she were a beauty. Or brought any great fortune to the marriage.

And if there were reservations about the character of the bridegroom, nonetheless no one had ever questioned the fastidiousness of his taste. So what, they patently wondered, could have drawn him to Juliet?

"Did you meet Mr. Langford before or after you came to London?" one aunt asked avidly.

"Just how did you manage to bring him up to scratch?" an uncle had the temerity to demand.

Mrs. Galsworth intervened, more because she feared that Lord or Lady Darton would overhear than out of any concern for Juliet's feelings.

"Nonsense!" she said, with an artificial laugh that could not help but grate on everyone's nerves. "There is no mystery here. Mr. Langford and Juliet met at Lady Merriweather's ball. They were instantly taken with one another. Mr. Galsworth and I should have preferred it had they been a trifle less impetuous, but what can one do when a young couple conceives an intense *tendre* for one another?"

More than one person grimaced at his or her neighbor but no one dared contradict Juliet's mother outright. Still, it was enough to put an end to the questioning, and for that, Juliet was grateful.

The whole affair was a sad trial to nearly everyone involved and nearly everyone, it might safely be said, felt a great degree of relief when it was time for them all to go home.

Home, to Juliet and James, was a hotel. But they saw little need to tell anyone that detail. Instead, when asked, they said they were going somewhere special. And while Juliet's parents were patently skeptical, they were not about to mar the triumph of their day by asking any questions it was clear neither James nor Juliet wished to answer.

But before they could entirely escape, Mr. Galsworth took James aside and said, emotion strong in his voice, "Juliet is my only chick. Mind you make her happy now or I shall call you to account, brother of a lord as you are or not!"

James looked directly at Galsworth so that the man could not doubt the sincerity of his reply. "If it is within my power I shall do so, and if it is not, you cannot chastise me more than I shall chastise myself."

They clasped hands then, friends now where before there had been only wary respect.

Chapter 10

James offered Juliet a glass of ratafia. Nervously she took it. Well, that was all right, he was rather nervous himself.

Still, he thought, looking around the elegantly appointed suite of rooms Woods had engaged for them for their wedding night, at least this matter had been taken care of in a most satisfactory way. Mind you, a certain solution had occurred to him concerning his engine and he would much rather have been trying to implement it. But James understood all too well that he could not abandon his bride tonight. No, nor even take her with him.

However much his own mind might be engaged in matters mechanical, he did understand enough to know that there were certain rituals that must be observed. And this was one of them. A generous supper had been laid out and James indicated the table now.

"Shall we eat?" he asked.

She smiled gratefully and he congratulated himself on finding just the right gentle tone with which to speak to his new bride. They sat opposite one another, conscious of the servants hovering about to serve them.

"It went off well today, I should think," James said as soup was placed before him.

"Yes, it did," Juliet agreed, her voice as stilted as his own.

She ignored the memory of Lady Darton condescending to her and of Lord Darton's disapproving scowl. She particularly ignored the memory of Mama attempting to ingratiate herself with both of them with a singular lack of success.

Instead, she said, somewhat timidly, "I liked your brothers Harry and Philip."

James smiled. "Yes, they are good fellows, aren't they? And I thought it very nice of Sir Thomas and Lady Levenger to attend."

"He is a distinguished judge, isn't he?" Juliet asked, desperate for something to say.

James recounted a little of his history. "In many ways Sir Thomas is an admirable man. His family was not quite the thing and he became a barrister both because it suited his temperament and because he needed some way to earn a living. He rose quickly and became King's Counsel at an exceptionally young age."

He paused, and then added with some constraint, "He and my father were dear friends. You will no doubt think that strange, considering the difference in their breeding, but as I once told you, my father was accounted a great reformer and he cared not a whit for such things. And when he died we discovered that Sir Thomas stood in some part as guardian to us. He has been all that is kind and we have benefited greatly from his counsel. I shall not cut the connection, now that we are married," he concluded a trifle defiantly. "Even Athenia has not been able to persuade George to do so! And you may as well know that I am acquainted with any number of individuals who are not acceptable to the *ton.*"

Juliet was shocked and it showed in her expression. "I should never ask you to cut the connection with anyone who was important to you," she said. Then, her temper rising, she went on, "You must have a very poor impression of me if you think I could be so foolish or so cruel. You may have whatever friends you wish and I shall not care one bit!"

And with that, to her great mortification, and his, Juliet burst into tears. Instantly, James was on his feet, waving the servants away and coming around to kneel by her chair. He took her hand in his and with the other stroked her hair.

"You must forgive me," James said gently. "I have no practice in this sort of thing."

She sniffed. "You? London's most notable bachelor? The joy of every hostess? Oh, yes, I have heard far more than I wished to hear about what a delightful gentleman you are. So don't give me such fustian as to say you don't know how to do the pretty, when it suits you!"

"Yes, but this is not doing the pretty," James retorted, with pardonable exasperation. "I am trying to comfort you, Juliet."

She blinked at him. "You are?"

"Well, what the devil did you think I was doing?" he demanded.

She blushed. "I don't know. I haven't any more experience than you do at these things," she confided naively. "Indeed, I daresay I have much less."

"Well, I am. And I am sorry for thinking you as . . . as high-handed or as snobbish as Athenia."

She sniffed again. "I cannot think how I have come to be such a watering pot, just now," she said, with mortification evident in her voice. "I do not mean to be and in general I never cry. It is most lowering that I should do so on my wedding day."

James smiled. "Do you think it possible," he asked coaxingly, "that it is precisely because it is your wedding day that you should do so? After all, this is a momentous occasion for the both of us and I must confess my own nerves are not altogether steady."

She smiled at him and he blinked. The transformation was, he thought, astonishing however many times he saw it, and as he did each time, he found himself once again silently vowing to give Juliet cause to smile as often as it was possible to do so.

Abruptly they both became aware of the interested and highly approving watchful gaze of the servants. James rose to his feet and cleared his throat.

"You may go," he said. "We shall finish serving ourselves."

Juliet touched his hand. "I am not really hungry," she said.

He nodded. "You may take everything away," he told the servants.

From the hastily suppressed grins, it was patent they put their own interpretation upon all of this!

But for Juliet and James, the reality was rather different. When they were alone he said, holding out a hand to her, "Come sit on the sofa. We have not truly had any time alone together, no chance to talk since the night you helped me work on my engine."

She came willingly. "How is your engine?" she asked eagerly. "Did you try the things I suggested?"

"I thought," he said diffidently, "you might wish to be there when I did."

Now her face really lit up. "Oh, I should!" she exclaimed.

She looked at him expectantly and James found himself at a loss as to how to proceed. "That is not precisely what I meant, however," he said, "when I said that we might wish to talk."

"Oh?"

There was such innocence in her gaze that James, who was uneasily aware of his own innocence, did not quite know what to say. Still, he tried.

"We have not talked of what to expect from this marriage of ours."

"Mama explained everything," Juliet said earnestly.

Then, as though realizing from his expression that perhaps she had been indiscreet, she added, "That is, you are quite right. We ought to talk. What did you wish to say?"

James closed his eyes and then opened them again. Why had he ever thought this would be easy? That Miss Galsworth would be sufficiently sensible that they would have no awkwardness between them?

"I wished to tell you," he said carefully, "that I shall do my best to try to put you at ease and do nothing to distress you."

"Oh. And I shall do my best to do the same for you," Juliet said brightly.

James closed his eyes again and silently counted to twenty. When he opened them, she was regarding him with a somewhat anxious gaze. He tried once more.

"There may be some awkwardness as we become accustomed to one another but we are both sensible people and I think we shall deal tolerably well together."

Still she did not seem to understand what it was he was trying to say. James was at a loss. He could not, he simply could not, bring himself to be any more explicit about the marriage bed. He would simply have to hope that matters worked themselves out naturally.

Perhaps, he thought, his mind taking another direction, he ought to reassure her about other matters as well. He did not wish her to think, after all, that he would be an overbearing husband, forever telling her what to do or attempting to dictate her interests. And it would not be an unreasonable fear on her part, particularly after Athenia's behavior at the wedding breakfast today.

"I do want to assure you that I shall not," he said earnestly, "interfere with your interests and I presume you are too sensible to interfere with mine."

"Oh."

This time there was no brightness in either her ex-

pression or her voice. She would not meet his eyes,
and utterly confused, James wondered what the devil
was wrong now?

He would not interfere with her interests and he
did not wish her to interfere with his. He had just said
so. Juliet had to fight back the tears that threatened
to spill out and trickle down her cheek.

This would never do! Mama had warned her, had
she not? Well, it was time Juliet heeded all the lessons
Mama had tried to give her over the years. If this was
how it was to be, why then she ought to remember
that it was apparently so for every other wife as well.
She would just have to find a way to bear her
unhappiness.

Juliet realized that James was gazing at her with
both concern and dismay in his expression. She forced
herself to smile and tried to reassure him.

"How very sensible of you!" she exclaimed.

She could hear his sigh of relief and perversely it
vexed her greatly. Determined to be sensible, she rose
to her feet and declared, "Well, I suppose there is no
point in putting off matters any longer. I shall prepare
for bed and you may join me shortly."

And what there was in those words to upset James
was beyond her ability to comprehend. Hadn't he just
said he expected and wished for her to be sensible?
Then what on earth was the matter with the man?
Whatever it was, she refused to upset herself and fled
to the other room to let Margaret help her out of her
clothes and into the nightshift Mama had ordered for
her for this night.

It was a measure of her distress that Juliet scarcely
noticed all the ruffles and ribbons that decorated the
dratted thing. Nor did she pay any attention to the
chatter of her maid.

What did she wish to hear of "enduring"? Or to be
told that perhaps it was not so bad after all, consider-

ing that one of Mama's kitchen girls had found herself in an interesting condition by choice?

Interesting condition! The thought suddenly assailed Juliet and her courage almost failed her. She was not, she told herself firmly, ready to find herself in an interesting condition and she was not, definitely not, going to allow it to happen to her just yet.

Which meant that perhaps, as soon as possible, she ought to ask Mama just how one avoided or perhaps it was chose to become in an interesting way. One wouldn't want it to happen by accident, after all.

It did occur to Juliet that James might know but somehow she did not quite feel equal to the task of asking him. Somehow she thought he might not wish her to do so and she had already upset him more than once since the ceremony today. No, she would wait and ask Mama.

It was astonishing, she thought, the number of things that were important and yet, unaccountably, had been omitted from her education.

At last Margaret had finished fussing over her and left the room with a backward anxious glance and a giggle. Juliet looked around, feeling more awkward than ever.

What ought she to do now? How would James expect her to be waiting for him? Margaret had wanted to tuck her up into bed and under the covers but that struck Juliet far too much like hiding. Perhaps she ought to sit on a chair near the fireplace? That seemed equally odd. Finally she settled for sitting on the edge of the bed, her feet planted firmly on the floor, her hands in her lap, clenched together to keep them from trembling.

That was how James found her.

James chose to change in the other room. Woods, the perfect gentleman's gentleman, made no comment as he helped his employer change into his dressing gown. Nor did he have the temerity to offer any advice. He must have known his employer would not appreciate his doing so.

After he was ready and had dismissed Woods for the night, still James hesitated. How long, he wondered, ought he to give Juliet to prepare herself? How long did ladies require, anyway?

Eventually he decided that he had probably waited long enough. James opened the bedroom door to find his bride sitting on the edge of the bed, regarding the doorway with wide, frightened eyes. Suddenly his own trepidations seemed utterly unimportant and his only concern was to put her at ease.

Closing the door behind him, he moved toward Juliet and drew her to her feet. This time he had no need to think about where to place his hands or how to tilt his head as he embraced his bride.

Somehow it was perfectly natural to hold her close and kiss her gently. Somehow it was perfectly natural for that kiss to deepen into something much more. And by the time they found themselves in bed, his dressing gown and her nightshift somehow discarded, both Juliet and James were far beyond the point of worrying how to do what was coming so very naturally to the both of them.

Mama was wrong, Juliet thought. What happened in the marriage bed was not something to be endured. Not in the least. It was something she rather thought she could come to enjoy a great deal. Indeed, she thought a moment later, she already did!

Chapter 11

⌒

Juliet woke to find herself alone. For a moment she wondered where she was, and then she recalled, with a sense of utter happiness, the night before. But where was her bridegroom?

Margaret, her maid, bustling into the room with morning tea, merely said, in reply to Juliet's question, "Oh, Mr. Langford went out an hour ago. He said to tell you he would be back later."

One could not press the girl for information she patently did not have. With a puzzled frown, Juliet sipped her tea and then dressed for the day in her plainest gown. She stared at the other dresses her maid had hung up and then made a decision.

"Margaret, we are going to take all the bows and ruffles and furbelows off every gown in my wardrobe! Or at least," she temporized, "some of them."

The maid's eyes went wide but she did not protest. Indeed, it would seem that at least a tiny part of her approved for she began to smile.

"Your mama won't like it," she warned.

Juliet fixed her maid with a determined gaze and said, "My mama has nothing to say to the matter, ever again. I am a married woman!"

"And Mr. Langford? Will he approve?" the maid asked, a trifle nervously.

For a moment, Juliet's resolve wavered. Then she

squared her shoulders. "Mr. Langford is a man. No doubt he won't even notice," she said.

The maid nodded vigorously. "That's true. Men never do, do they? Where shall we begin?"

James met Sir Thomas Levenger on the street in front of Philip's house. "You were called here, too, sir?" he asked in confusion.

Sir Thomas quirked an eyebrow and shrugged. "We shall find out in due course the reason for our summons. Meanwhile, we do not wish everyone on the street to note our presence and wonder at it. Inside, m'boy, inside!"

The footman betrayed nothing by his expression as he showed the two gentlemen into the study. There, James's older brother, Philip, was waiting for them, and Harry.

"So, Harry," Sir Thomas said gruffly, even as his shrewd eyes took in every detail of the younger man's appearance, "Do you mean to tell us the truth today about why they've given you leave? And about how things are going at the front?"

Major Harry Langford's expression turned grim. He waved them all to seats then looked at Philip, who nodded and quietly locked the study door. He waited for him to sit down again behind the study desk, which was piled high with law books.

"Harry has a request to make of us," Philip said.

The major, the only one still on his feet, regarded each of them carefully. He stood with his legs braced wide apart, his hands clasped behind his back.

To Sir Thomas he said, "You ask how things are at the front. Not going nearly as well as we should wish. I am here, ostensibly because of James's entanglement with a young woman, the woman he married yesterday. Congratulations, by the way, James. I think she will suit you perfectly. That was certainly my excuse to George. But the real reason I am here is that I need your help. All of you—I shall need your help, if you will give it."

He paused, as though not entirely certain how to go on. He looked at each man in the room and each man in turn nodded and murmured, "Of course."

Harry's shoulders relaxed just a trifle. "We must find a better, faster way of sending information from England to the continent," he said.

"I have been experimenting with lights and lenses," James said slowly. "If you can get the information to the coast, I can think of a possible way to get it across the channel without any delay. I think it would work, though I should have to run some experiments to be sure. But, Harry, those on the other side will all be able to see it, regardless of which army they represent, and your man would have to be in French territory, which would be very risky."

Harry grinned. "I thought you might have some notions, James."

"A code," Philip said thoughtfully, "would remove the problem of the enemy intercepting the message. It ought to be based on a common book. Perhaps the Bible? Do you carry one with you?"

"Not yet, but I will, if it comes to that," Harry said with a grin. "Many men do and it would arouse no comment. But there is still the matter of getting the information to the coast and James's system of lights and lenses."

"My possible system," James cautioned.

Harry waved a hand as though to dismiss the possibility of failure. "You'll find a way," he said. "But how do we get the information to the coast? Sir Thomas, have you any suggestions?"

The elder fellow hesitated, and when he finally did speak, there was something of a twinkle in his shrewd eyes as he said, succinctly, "Mrs. Philip Langford."

"Emily?"

"Does she not write for a newspaper?" Sir Thomas

asked, completely unruffled by the exclamations this statement produced.

Philip colored up, trying to ignore the stares and questions his brothers were asking. "I, er, what makes you think that?" he began. Then, with a sigh of resignation, he added, "Lady Levenger."

Sir Thomas nodded gravely. "Lady Levenger," he agreed. "Agatha is, after all, your wife's aunt and she is accustomed to confide in her. You need not fear, however, that any of us in this room will give away her secret. We have all known for some time, after all. Except perhaps Harry. But I do think it may be the answer to the present quandary."

"How so?" Harry asked.

"I think I know," Philip replied. "If she puts the message in her writing, then anyone who gets the paper can transmit the message with James's system of lights and lenses, am I right?"

Sir Thomas nodded. "The importance, I presume, is that no one should know a message is being sent to the coast. Messengers can too easily be intercepted. But no one would think anything of someone having a newspaper delivered. Not even if he sent to London for it every day. I know, and you must as well, men who do so whenever they are out of the city for any length of time."

The Langford brothers nodded. Harry tapped his chin thoughtfully. "How often does your wife's writing appear in the paper?" he asked.

Philip hesitated. "At least once a week. More if she wished. But we have not wanted it to overwhelm our lives. How often would you need her to write something?"

Harry considered the question carefully. "Once a week would probably be sufficient. I must arrange for information to be given to her in time for her to include it in her writing, and we must decide how our man on the coast would know what it was that he was to take as the message to transmit. And I must choose someone to go to the coast."

"I shall have to go anyway, to test my ideas," James said instantly. "I could take my wife there, claiming it to be our honeymoon journey. You will need to place a man on the other side to receive the message and we shall need a means to know if it has been safely received."

"I can arrange for someone, temporarily to do so," Harry said slowly. "Then when I go back across the channel, I can check matters out myself. I should like to work out as many details, arrange for all possible contingencies, before I leave. I shall not be able to return for some time. So let us figure out every possible thing that could go wrong, every possible detail we must get right."

For the next several hours, the men were engaged in doing precisely that. Had they been able to see Emily and Juliet, they might, at least two of them, have felt some trepidation. But as is usually the case in such situations, it was fortunate that they did not.

Juliet was feeling more than a trifle let down when her husband had still not returned by late morning. Perhaps that was why she was so delighted when her sister-in-law was announced.

"Pray call me Emily!" Mrs. Philip Langford told Juliet, reaching out her hands.

Juliet took them, not knowing what else to do. Or what else to say. So she smiled. "And I pray you will call me Juliet."

The other woman sat down, her eyes dancing as she said, "You are wondering why I should be intruding on you just a day after your wedding but I know, you see, that our husbands are together—indeed, I have been banished from my own house—and we are likely to have some time alone."

She paused, as though not certain how to go on,

but then she took a deep breath and said, "Yesterday I saw how Lord and Lady Darton treated you and I wished to come and tell you to pay them no mind. I don't, I assure you, and they were no more pleased by my marriage to Philip than they are with yours to James. But as I told you yesterday, I think that you and I shall deal famously together. Neither of us are conventional ladies and we shall need to stand by one another, don't you think?"

Juliet blinked, almost overwhelmed by her new sister-in-law. But then she smiled again, her mind made up.

"I think we shall deal extremely well together," she replied. "At least I hope we will. And if you truly wish to do me a service, I pray you will tell me about James."

It was Emily's turn to look taken aback. "Tell you what?" she asked.

Juliet steeled herself to honesty, however foolish it might make her appear. "You will no doubt think it an odd request, but James and I were married after only the briefest of acquaintances. And yet I mean to make this marriage work. But to do so I must learn everything I can about my husband. And therefore I should be grateful for any detail, however small, that you can tell me about him."

"Of course I shall help you," Emily vowed. Then, impulsively she leaned forward and hugged Juliet. "Oh, I do like you, Juliet! I thought I should, from the moment I heard you give Athenia, that is to say Lady Darton, a setdown at your wedding breakfast."

Juliet caught her lower lip between her teeth. "That was not very well done of me," she confessed.

"No, but so vastly entertaining," Emily said, her eyes dancing with amusement. "And so irresistible. I have been wanting to do so ever since I met her."

"I suppose," Juliet said slowly, "that Lord Darton

was even more mortified by his father's conduct than any of his brothers."

"You know about the late Lord Darton?" Emily asked with some surprise.

"It is the one thing I do know," Juliet replied. "I know that he was a reformer, a rebellious fellow who flouted all conventions, and the family was ostracized because of it."

"And then he and Lady Darton were killed in a carriage accident some nine years ago," Emily added. "His conduct, and the consequences, has affected all of them. As you say, Lord Darton, as the eldest, took it most to heart. He lives his life in such a way that no one can say he is like his father was and he chose a wife as conventional as he. Even my own dear Philip," Emily said with a mischievous grin, "was a trifle too inclined toward convention when I first met him."

"And Sir Thomas and Lady Levenger?" Juliet asked. "I collect they are very close to the family."

"Lord and Lady Darton's death left the brothers on their own at much too young an age," Emily said. "I collect that Sir Thomas has stood in some sort as guardian to them ever since. He was, you see, a close friend to the late Lord Darton. As for Lady Levenger, she is my aunt and so Philip and I are doubly close to both of them."

"I wonder if I shall ever know the family as well as you do," Juliet said, with something of a sigh.

"You shall," Emily assured her. She paused and looked at Juliet shrewdly. "Is there anything else you wish me to tell you?"

Juliet hesitated, blushed, then straightened her shoulders and said fiercely, "Tell me how I can make him fall in love with me! Tell me how I can please James so that he never wishes to have female friends, as Mama has sworn he will. Tell me how I can please him as well as any member of the demimonde!"

Emily gasped, then laughed. "Good heavens! You are indeed unconventional!" she exclaimed unsteadily. "Even more so than I."

All the fierceness seemed to go out of Juliet. "I have shocked you," she said with dismay.

Emily shook her head. "No! I am pleased. But I do not quite know how to help you. However," she said, thoughtfully, "I have a notion. There are some books in Philip's library that might perhaps help. They seem to have the oddest pictures, and when once he found me holding one and looking at it, quite by accident, I assure you, he told me it was most improper. But if you wish to be improper, I can think of nothing that could be more useful, can you?"

Her eyes wide, Juliet shook her head. Then, with a grin she said, "Oh, I do like you, Emily! And I am so glad you came to call upon me today! How soon can you bring one of these books?"

Chapter 12

～

James did not think to explain to his bride either where he had been or the reason behind his announcement that they were probably going to go the coast for their honeymoon. His only awkwardness came when he had to tell her that he wasn't quite certain when they would be leaving.

Nor did he notice a certain preoccupation on her part. Juliet was subdued, but surely that was proper for a wife? After all, had he not called her sensible?

When she ventured to ask whether he was thinking of his engine, James did condescend to admit to her, "Well, actually, I am thinking of something rather different, at the moment. I am trying to solve a rather interesting problem involving lenses and lights."

"In what way?" Juliet asked.

How much did he dare tell her? Perhaps just a little?

"Oh, to send signals some distance."

"At night, you mean?"

Bless her, she was quick! "Yes," James agreed eagerly, "at night or in bad weather. Modulated signals, you understand."

"What do you intend to try first?"

He told her. Harry might think him indiscreet, but the luxury of having someone to discuss his experiments with was one he found he simply could not

deny himself. And so he told her, consoling himself
that at least she did not know, could not guess the
purpose at hand.

Certainly the questions Juliet asked were sensible
ones and helped James clarify his own thoughts. So
long as he did not explain to her why he was working on the problem, his brothers could not mind his
confiding in her, could they? After all, it was not as
though she, a lady, could speak of this to anyone
else.

So James spent a surprisingly agreeable evening
with his bride. And if her eyes glittered suspiciously,
he simply presumed she was tired and never guessed
that it was from tears threatening to spill out.

Nor did he realize how upset he made her when he
said, "You had best go to bed now, Juliet. I shall be
awake for some time working on this problem. But
you needn't fear I shall disturb you when I come to
bed."

After all, if she had been upset, she would have
said something, wouldn't she? Isn't that how a sensible
woman would behave?

Juliet tried to keep her face impassive as her maid
undressed her for bed. She tried to pretend nothing
was amiss. She didn't think she entirely succeeded,
for Margaret kept looking at her with a concerned
expression in her eyes. But Juliet did her best. After
all, it would be truly humiliating for even the servants
to know how little her husband cared for her
company.

But when she was alone, sitting in her dressing gown
by the empty fireplace, Juliet gave vent to her emotions. Tears rolled down her cheeks and her body
shook with sobs she fought to keep silent. She did not
think she could bear it if anyone overheard and came
in to see what was wrong!

To be sure, she was glad James wished to share with

her his experiments. But it was only one day after they had married. Could he not think, even a little, of her? Could he not wish, even a little, to kiss or embrace her? Was she truly such an antidote, after all?

Still, she was not a woman given to self-pity. When the tears had run their course, a very short time later, Juliet sniffed, dried her face, and set her mind to how she could turn matters about.

Emily had promised to bring books as soon as might be but surely she need not wait for that? Surely there was something she could do beforehand? Ought she to go out to the other room? Ought she to go and find James?

A moment's reflection decided her against such an action. She knew only too well how vexed she would be if someone interrupted her when she was in the midst of trying to fix a carriage or a pump or some such thing.

Well, perhaps she should stay awake until he came to bed. Perhaps then, if he found her awake and willing, he would be open to the notion of repeating what they had done the night before.

Mama would say that what she contemplated was scandalously forward and could only give her husband a disgust of her. But if James already had a disgust of her—and he certainly did not seem to want her company tonight—then what could she possibly have to lose?

So Juliet glanced in the looking glass to make certain she had wiped away all trace of her tears and then removed her dressing gown so that she could climb between the sheets. She must pretend to be asleep, she told herself, so that James did not retreat from the room before she could set her plan into motion. That meant she must blow out the candle and wait in the dark.

Unless, perhaps, she could feign having fallen asleep

with it still lit? Unless she could pretend she had been waiting for him and fallen asleep?

In the end, that was what Juliet decided to do.

James yawned. What hour of the clock was it? That late! Well, he'd best get some sleep. His brothers were expecting him to meet with them again in the morning.

Quietly, so as not to disturb Juliet, for it would be unconscionable to rob her of sleep as well, James tiptoed into the bedroom, careful to make no noise as he disrobed. Then he set his candle on the night stand and blew it out before slipping between the sheets.

Her candle guttered low and he was about to blow it out when it went out of its own accord. James frowned. He would have to speak to Juliet about such a dangerous habit. One really ought not to leave a candle burning when one went to sleep.

The image of Juliet sound asleep was so clear in his mind that James jumped when he felt her hand brush his groin. Instantly it was gone. He would have thought he imagined it, so brief was the touch, except that his body had reacted unmistakably.

He stared at her suspiciously.

She murmured in her sleep and turned toward him, but her eyes were closed. Could he have been mistaken? She did seem sound asleep now.

Softly he said, "Juliet?"

This time she blinked her eyes sleepily, and said, with a puzzled frown, "James?"

He sighed. It must have been his imagination. His wife could not possibly have touched him as he thought she had. At least not with any awareness of doing so. He was a brute to have wakened her.

"Nothing," he said. "Go back to sleep."

And with that, to keep her from realizing the state of his arousal and to avoid temptation, he turned away from her. Was that a sniff, behind his back? Surely not. It had to be his imagination. He really must do something about it, his imagination, that is, one of these days. Meanwhile, they both needed to sleep.

Only he couldn't sleep. Not when her body moved closer to his. Not when he could feel her breath on his back, even though she was careful not to touch him.

Was she trying to arouse him?

No, surely not. She was asleep. And in any event, Juliet was a lady! But it was most distracting and definitely not conducive to sleeping.

He tried to edge away. She moved closer. He could go no farther without falling out of bed. This was impossible! He was going to have to get up or he was likely to ravish her as she slept, for all he could think of was how she had felt in his arms the night before!

Quietly, and as gently as he could, James tried to swing his feet to the floor. Before he could accomplish this simple maneuver, however, a hand reached out and grabbed a fistful of his nightshirt. A nightshirt he was wearing out of deference to Juliet's modesty. But it was her voice that snared him even tighter.

"James? Please don't go."

He turned, even as the fist let go of his nightshirt and he found himself gazing down into wide-open, half-frightened eyes.

"Have you had a nightmare?" he asked, his mind ever practical.

She shook her head.

"I noticed you left your candle burning. Are you afraid of the dark?" he persisted.

She shook her head again.

"Then what," he asked with pardonable exasperation, "is the problem?"

Even in the dark he could feel her blush. It was something about the way she averted her eyes and seemed to shrink in upon herself.

He had to bend forward to hear her as she whispered, "I, that is, will you make love with me, James? I rather liked it last night."

James felt as though a heavy weight had fallen on his chest and he could scarcely breathe. She wanted to make love? She wished him to kiss her and hold her and do what they had done last night?

His voice came out as something of a squeak as he tried to reply. "I, er, that is, of course, if that is what you wish, Juliet."

This time she nodded vigorously, leaving him in no doubt that it was. And so, with a sigh of relief and, if truth be known, delight, James reached for his bride and made love with her, thinking all the while, that he must be the most fortunate man in creation!

In another part of town, Sir Thomas Levenger reached for a sheet of paper and dipped his pen into the inkwell. Perhaps he ought to ask the major first, but there was so little time. If they were to help Harry as he had asked, Sir Thomas strongly suspected they would need the help of an old friend of his, Frederick Baines.

No one quite knew just what Frederick Baines did, but somehow there were always rumors. And Sir Thomas knew for a fact that Baines had been of great service to their country, more than once. Added to that, the man had a clever mind, a kind heart, and an ability to see things others did not see. He would be invaluable to Harry's plans.

So Sir Thomas dipped his pen again and began to write. Time enough in the morning to tell the major what he had done. Particularly as Sir Thomas was far too shrewd to commit anything to paper that ought not to be seen by other eyes. No, anyone reading this missive would only think that the elder barrister was lonely for the company of an old friend.

Which he was. A smile began to play about Sir Thomas's mouth. Even if Harry decreed Baines was not to be brought into the plan, it would be fun to have Baines in London again. The man knew the most astonishing people and precisely how to ferret out the most entertaining places.

When the letter was written and folded and sealed, Sir Thomas set it on the pile of correspondence that was to be sent out in the morning. Then he blew out the candle and sought his bed.

It was late and he was tired, but somehow he was not surprised to find Agatha awake and waiting for him, a tender smile upon her face that he had come to know and love so well.

"We are, you know, a most unfashionable couple," he told her sternly.

She was not in the least abashed. "How so?" she demanded teasingly.

He held his arms open and she came without hesitation straight into them. Sir Thomas kissed the top of her head. "We are unfashionable because we love one another so dearly. What a shocking thing, after all!"

Agatha turned her face up to his, a teasing smile playing about her mouth. "Do you know, dear, I think I rather like being shocking," she said.

With a tiny crow of triumph he captured her lips with his. "So do I, my love," he said between kisses. "So do I."

Chapter 13

Juliet woke the next morning certain that today would be wonderful and far different from yesterday. How could it not be, after last night? Unfortunately her happy spirits lasted only as long as it took her to discover that once again she had been left on her own, with no notion when her husband planned to return. He had left a note with some funds telling her to go shopping if she wished, but that was a poor substitute for his company.

Indeed, the morning felt very much like a reenactment of the day before. Even the arrival of Emily seemed to prove it was so. She had to blink fiercely to contain the distress she felt at the sight of her new friend.

"Are you abandoned again as well, this morning?" Juliet asked, unable to keep the bitterness entirely out of her voice.

Emily tilted her head to one side. She glanced around to be certain that there were no servants about before she answered.

"You must understand that my husband and yours and their brother Harry are remarkably close. I fear it will always be so. It is not that they do not care about us, but that they are sworn to one another whenever there is a need. And apparently there is a need. No doubt Philip will tell me in time what it is.

Meanwhile, it gives us the chance to be alone together again and for me to share with you one of the books I found in Philip's library. It is the oddest thing! There are pictures and such bound between the pages of otherwise entirely unexceptionable text."

Her worst fears momentarily forgotten, Juliet's interest was caught and she leaned forward to see. As they turned the pages of the book Emily had brought, she shyly told Emily what she had attempted.

"And I was certain he liked it," Juliet said, a hint of desperation in her voice. "But still he was gone when I woke and he did not trouble to leave me word of when he would be back."

Emily patted her hand soothingly. "He is a man and men are, in general, remarkably thoughtless about such things. I daresay he has no notion you are even distressed. From what you have told me, he no doubt believes you are glad for the time to yourself."

"Well, I am not glad for it!" Juliet countered with patent annoyance.

"Of course not," Emily agreed, not troubling to hide her amusement. "I only meant that it is what he is likely to believe. He is, after all, a man."

That mollified Juliet a trifle. And besides, the pictures in the books were absolutely fascinating. At one point she and Emily turned the book first sideways and then the other way again. Then they looked at one another.

"Do you really think such a position is possible?" Emily asked doubtfully.

"I don't know," Juliet countered, "but wouldn't it be interesting to try and find out?"

That provoked such gales of laughter between the two ladies that Juliet's maid nervously tapped on the door and then poked her head in to ask if there was anything her mistress required.

Which only set off fresh gales of laughter and a fear, on Margaret's part, that her mistress was in a fair way to losing her mind. And if she did, Margaret thought angrily, it would all be the master's fault and serve him right for leaving her poor mistress alone like this!

The Langford brothers, Harry and James, were bent over sketches that James was making. They were in Philip's study, but he wasn't there. He had a case before the bench today and Sir Thomas was hearing another.

"I think I had best take you to my workshop," James said at last. "It will be easier if I show you some of the lenses and lights I have been experimenting with, and by the time we return, Philip may be here and can tell us if he has spoken with his wife."

Harry nodded. "Excellent notion. Besides, I have long been curious to see this mysterious workshop of yours. Ever since Philip told me it existed."

Their plans were forestalled, however, by the sudden arrival of Lord Darton.

"George!" both brothers said, with a marked lack of enthusiasm.

"Harry. James. What the devil are you doing here? I came to see Philip and am told he is before the bar today and that the two of you are here. Why Philip must needs be a barrister is beyond me and that he actually wishes to work at the profession is completely absurd. I wish the two of you would tell him so! At least the two of you are gentlemen though, James, I wish you would gamble a trifle less and, Harry, I wish your profession less hazardous."

James and Harry looked at one another and schooled their expressions to innocence.

"Yes, George," they said meekly.

But Lord Darton was not deceived. He snorted. "Neither of you shows the least respect toward me, even though I am head of the family. Very well, if Philip is not here, I shall have to come back later."

"Perhaps one of us could be of help?" James suggested.

"No, no. It is merely some absurd rumor I heard that his wife is writing for a newspaper. Nonsense, of course! Still, I thought I ought to warn him."

"But why should anyone think she is?" James protested, careful not to catch Harry's eye.

George sighed. "It seems someone has let slip that a female is writing for one of the papers, and since of late there have been some attacks on institutions Philip's wife has been known to ring a peal about, she is suspect. Some of the words, it is said, sound remarkably like hers."

"Coincidence?" James suggested.

"No doubt," Darton agreed, "but a problem all the same. These rumors must be stopped!"

"You are quite right," Harry said soothingly. "When we see Philip we'll tell him about this calumny. You're quite right that he ought to know and ought to take steps to nip the rumor in the bud."

Darton looked at his younger brother with some surprise. "That's very handsome of you, Harry. Very handsome indeed. Good. Well, then, I shall be going. Mind you don't forget to tell him."

"We won't!" Harry said fervently.

When they were alone again, James eyed his brother and the major answered his unspoken question. "Of course we don't want anyone to know Emily is writing for the paper. We don't want anyone to make that sort of connection. Particularly not if she is going to be putting information into her writing for us."

"But how do we counter the rumors?" James asked.

"I don't know," Harry replied. "But one way or another we must."

"Perhaps we should go and find Philip?" James suggested. "And tell him what George has said."

Harry shook his head. "No, we don't want to draw

attention to ourselves in such a way. Time enough to
tell him tonight, if he has not heard by then. In the
mean time, why don't you show me your workshop
and the experiments you have been doing?"

Nothing could have appealed to James more, and
within minutes, they were on their way.

Sir Thomas frowned, causing the counsel pleading the
case before him to quake. Had he somehow offended
the judge? Made a fatal error in his presentation?

But Sir Thomas's frown had nothing to do with the
case in hand. Instead he was thinking of Frederick
Baines again. There would be no better person to help
with Major Langford's project. If he would come. Sir
Thomas wished it had been possible to convey more
of the urgency of the matter in his letter and he found
himself rewriting the blasted thing in his mind.

"M'lud?"

That brought Sir Thomas back to himself with a
start. He must not let his attention wander! This was,
as they all were, a case he took seriously. He made
the counsel repeat his last few statements and then
the case continued as it should. Despite his momentary lapse, Sir Thomas listened and dispensed justice
with his usual care.

Emily stared at Juliet's wardrobe. "I think," she
said quietly, "I should take you shopping."

"We did remove many of the bows and ruffles and
furbelows," Juliet said timidly.

"And that is a great improvement," Emily agreed.
"But the colors are still insipid. You would do better
with bolder shades and with somewhat different lines
in the cut of your clothes. I know a lady. She is not
one of the popular modistes, but she is working to
support herself and she has a wonderful eye. What do
you think? Are you willing to let her try?"

Juliet smiled and gave a great sigh of relief. "I

should like it above all things!" she said. "I was used to be overwhelmed by the modiste Mama chose. She spoke as if I were a green girl without the slightest notion what would suit me. As if she were vastly superior to either Mama or myself. I think I should much prefer a woman who would listen to what I have to say."

Emily grinned. "Good! Let us go at once. I promise you shall like her and she shall like you. My carriage should be here by now and I shall direct the coachman to take us to her home, where she works."

It took only a few moments for Juliet to gather her spencer and bonnet and gloves and reticule. Once they were settled in the carriage and headed for a part of London few ladies visited, Emily spoke again.

"I ought, perhaps, to tell you," she said hesitantly, "that this woman is someone who used to be in Bedlam. Not because she was mad but because her husband was angry with her. I have helped her to get out and away from the brute. And I throw whatever business I can her way, but only with ladies whom I know will not betray her secret. And she hires young girls to help her who have nowhere else to go, no other way to support themselves save by taking to the streets. Some of them, I think, perhaps even did for a while. If you wish, we may turn around and go back home."

Juliet squeezed Emily's hand. "Not for the world!" she said. "The poor woman! I should like to do something to help her. And if she is as good with a needle as you say, I shall be even more glad to give her my custom."

"Good, for we are here. Come, ignore the way this place appears and follow me. I assure you that Mrs. Wise will please you."

A word to the coachman and they made their way to a nearby building. Emily went up the stairs first, and while a number of the inhabitants of the building stared at them, no one tried to bar their way. Still, Juliet felt a trifle overwhelmed. Until, that is, a matronly woman opened her door at Emily's knock.

"Mrs. Langford! I didn't look to see you back here again so soon!"

"I've brought a customer for you," Emily said, stepping back to introduce Juliet. "Another Mrs. Langford. Mrs. James Langford."

Mrs. Wise bobbed a curtsey and said, "You are most welcome, ma'am. If you will come in?"

Juliet was relieved to see that despite the squalor of the neighborhood outside, the woman kept her own apartment as neat as a pin. And the three young women in the room were dressed neatly as well.

Mrs. Wise regarded Juliet with a shrewd eye and asked, "How may I help you, ma'am?"

Juliet looked down at her gown wryly. "My mother has dressed me in pale colors and insisted that every gown be covered with bows and furbelows. Now that I am married, I have done my best to remove the trim, but I think an even greater change is warranted."

"Bolder colors, I told her," Emily chimed in.

Mrs. Wise circled Juliet slowly. She studied her face. Finally, tapping her chin thoughtfully, she said, "Plain lines suit you. But not cut in quite this way. Deep, rich colors will bring out the color in your eyes."

Mrs. Wise drew out a sheaf of paper and began to sketch quickly. When she was done, she showed Juliet. "This for day, I think. And this, if you should be needing a ball gown. And this for a riding habit. This is what I should make, if I had the dressing of you."

Juliet let out the breath she didn't even know she had been holding. The sketches seemed to come to life, despite how quickly they had been drawn, and she could imagine herself happily wearing any one of the dresses Mrs. Wise had sketched for her.

"Oh, yes!" she said. "How soon can you begin?"

Mrs. Wise looked at Emily. "For a friend of Mrs.

Langford, I can begin today!" Then, a trifle diffidently she added, "I'm afraid I must ask for some funds in advance. To purchase the materials, you understand. I am still not as beforehand with the world as I should like."

It was clear how much it had cost Mrs. Wise to say those words. Impulsively Juliet opened her reticule and said, "Just tell me how much in funds you need to begin."

The matter was soon settled and Juliet and Emily in the carriage and on their way back to the hotel where Juliet and James were still staying.

"I wonder if he will be back there yet," Juliet said, more to herself than anyone else.

Emily patted her hand. "If not, you must not fall prey to the megrims. You've a lifetime ahead to turn your husband's attention to you. Contemplate instead your mama's astonishment the first time she sees you in the gowns Mrs. Wise is making for you."

Juliet grinned. "She will be mad as fire! And for the first time in my life, I shall feel as if I am almost pretty. I am so glad you took me to see Mrs. Wise. She understands perfectly."

Her smile faltered, however, as she said, "Was she truly in Bedlam? I cannot think it right that she should have ever been, for she was not in the least wanting in wits."

"Unfortunately she was indeed there," Emily said, her own expression grim. "And I, too, felt she was not wanting in wits. That was why I got her out. But as horrible as it was for her, at least in Bedlam she was safe from her beast of a husband. Too many women never are. 'Tis one reason she rescues girls from the streets and tries to teach them to assist her. Most leave and the ones who stay are not always the most skilled with a needle, but she will not give up."

"I am glad she does so," Juliet said with a fierceness

that surprised both of them. "It is not right that men should have such power over us."

"No," Emily agreed slowly. "But that is how it is. For now. We are fortunate in our husbands and ought to do what we can for those women we know who are not."

Chapter 14

～

Philip and Emily and Sir Thomas and Harry and James and another gentleman bent over the newspaper. They carefully read her latest piece and then consulted the Latin Bible they had borrowed from Lord Darton's library.

"Did I get it right?" Emily asked anxiously.

It took another ten minutes and then Sir Thomas and Harry grinned at one another.

"Perfect!" Harry said. "Absolutely perfect! And no one, reading it, could think anything amiss."

"Yes, but now you shall have to carry that heavy Latin Bible about," Philip said doubtfully.

Harry shrugged, his devil-may-care eyes dancing with amusement. "A good many men carry Bibles into battle," he said. "But if need be, perhaps I shall become a wandering priest, or something of the sort. I shall pretend that my whole life revolves around this Bible. Which, in a sense, it will."

James snorted. "As though anyone would believe such a thing of you!" he said.

Sir Thomas, however, eyed Harry thoughtfully. "That might not be such a bad notion," he said.

Harry rolled his eyes. "I was jesting," he said. "No more than James do I think anyone would believe me in such a role! Nor that Wellington would spare me from the fighting for such a purpose."

Now it was Sir Thomas who shrugged. "Perhaps. But should it ever come to that, it would make an excellent disguise. No one pays any attention to priests in wartime. What do you think, Baines?" he asked the other gentleman.

Frederick Baines smiled lazily. "I think young Harry would make an interesting priest but I am more concerned with this code you've come up with. And how to protect Mrs. Langford from discovery. You said there had been rumors that she is the author of several columns. How is her writing being delivered to the paper?"

Sir Thomas looked at Philip and Emily and quirked an eyebrow enquiringly.

"I send it with a footman to the paper," he said blankly. "But the fellow is never in livery when he goes."

"No, but perhaps he talks," Baines pointed out, with a deceptively careless air. "If you gave it instead to Sir Thomas and he chose, quite at random of course, a street urchin to send it with, that might be safer."

"But how can we be certain it will get there, then?" Emily blurted out.

"Oh, I think perhaps Harry could arrange that the right sort of urchin would be hanging about at the right time," Baines said blandly. "Couldn't you, Major Langford?"

Harry nodded slowly. A grin spread across his face. "Yes, I believe I could," he agreed.

"And then we must hint that another lady is responsible," Baines persisted. "I know one or two who might be amenable to being thought the author of Mrs. Langford's fiery pieces demanding reform."

There were a few more details to be worked out, but by the time the clock struck the hour, it was done.

"When will you return to the continent?" Philip asked.

"Very soon," Harry replied. "There is a great deal to do and not much time to do it in. James, you must be in place as soon as possible. Establish yourself and your wife as a newlywed pair absorbed entirely in one another. An eccentric who likes to tramp around the tops of cliffs and explore towers. All sorts of towers. There should also soon be a man in place in France. With luck you will both be able to do what you must without arousing local suspicion. Once I have word of success, I shall be off."

"And if this invention does not work?" Frederick Baines hazarded lightly.

Harry, Philip, and Sir Thomas smiled as one. James looked affronted. He would have protested but Sir Thomas forestalled him, "Oh, it will, Freddy. Trust me, or rather, trust James to see to that."

The men all rose to their feet and prepared to take their leave of one another. Frederick Baines promised to provide further advice at any time it was needed. Only he and Major Langford and James knew what else he was going to do. They all agreed that the fewer who knew the entire plan, the better it would be.

"Thank you, sir," Harry said, regarding the older man steadily. "They still speak of your exploits in the Mediterranean, you know, and have the highest regard for your abilities. They say it is a pity you chose to retire. I am grateful for the assistance you have given me."

Sir Thomas and Baines exchanged a look. Baines shrugged. "Life does not always turn out as one wishes. Remember that when you are on one of your own missions, m'boy!"

"I shall."

"Enough!" Sir Thomas said. "We must be going. And not all at once. We shall leave by different doors and at different times."

"Is that really necessary?" James asked. "Juliet will be anxious, wondering where I am."

The others regarded him with some amusement. "Do we really wish to find out?" Harry countered. "It is an easy enough precaution to take and if unneeded there is no harm done. But if anyone is watching the house, well, I should like to think we would be able to outwit them. But certainly you may leave first."

James made no more objection. Nor did the others. They moved to a small room off the foyer from which they could leave when Harry directed them to do so.

Philip remained in the study with his wife. What his servants thought of the odd goings-on, he did not care to question too closely. Instead, when the others were gone, he drew Emily onto his lap.

"So my love," he said, tracing a pattern on the back of her hand. "What do you think of becoming a spy?"

She brushed away the finger and pretended disdain. "I am nothing of the sort. Merely a . . . a conduit for information, I should say! And if I can be of help to your brothers, why, I am happy to do so, of course."

"How about of help to me?" Philip whispered, nibbling at her ear.

Emily laughed and wrapped her arms around his neck. "I think that could be arranged," she replied solemnly.

And if what followed might, by some, have been considered scandalous, well, Emily and Philip were married and it was no business of anyone else, anyway!

In the other room, as Sir Thomas and Frederick Baines patiently waited their turns to leave, their thoughts were very far from Emily and Philip. Harry was talking quietly with James in the foyer and no one was paying the slightest attention to them.

Sir Thomas said. "Am I correct in guessing, Freddy, that you will go yourself to the coast?"

Baines hesitated, then nodded. "I ought to have known you would guess! Yes, I am leaving tonight. I shall assist James with his experiments and guard his back, if need be. When we know that all is working well, then I shall take his place in sending out the signals. Eventually I shall find someone to replace me, but not until we are certain that all is going as it should."

"I wish others would value you as they should," Sir Thomas said with a heavy sigh.

A grim look formed at the corners of the other man's mouth. "It is enough," he said, "that those whose opinions I value do so. As for the others, well, I am who I am and will answer to no one for it."

There was no time to say more for Harry was signaling them that it was Frederick Baines's turn to leave. He clapped his hat onto his head, drew on his gloves, and with a wry smile sallied forth. Sir Thomas watched him from the window. He could think of no man he would trust more to watch over James or to assist in Harry's latest project.

It was just as well that he was the first to leave, James thought, as he hurried into the hotel where he and Juliet were still staying. He was tired and he missed his wife. It was a most unsettling notion, but nevertheless he did.

He paused in the doorway of the small sitting room of their suite and watched her pace before the empty fireplace. Something was different about her appearance and it took him a moment to realize what it might be.

"Is that a new dress?" he asked.

She started and whirled around to face him. Now what was there to cause her to color up in such a way?

"Yes. Do you like it?" she asked.

James could not understand why she should be nervous but he could see that she was. He moved forward and smiled reassuringly. "Very much," he said. "You should always dress in such bold colors and in such a

style. It is very much out of the common way. Who
was the modiste?"

Now she colored even more and muttered a name
he could not quite hear. When James frowned and
asked her to repeat it, Juliet fluttered her hands and
said, "Her name is Mrs. Wise. I collect she is new to
this business but I think she has a remarkable eye.
She has also had a difficult life and I should like to
help her. If you do not mind."

"Patronize whomever you wish," James said, thoroughly bewildered by now. "If Mrs. Wise can rig you
out this beautifully, then I should indeed think you
would wish to continue to have her make your gowns.
And of course you may help her if you wish. Indeed,
your generous heart is one of the things I most admire
about you, Juliet."

For a moment she smiled. Indeed, she looked quite
happy, James thought. And then her smile crumpled
to be replaced by a look of dismay. "You think I
looked an antidote before, don't you?" she said.

James blinked. He did not at once answer for he
had the notion that whatever he said would only upset
her more. "Why should you think such a thing?" he
asked at last.

Juliet sank onto the nearest chair and clasped her
hands in her lap, looking for all the world like a young
schoolgirl. She took a deep breath and met his gaze
squarely.

"Because each morning I rise and you are gone.
And I am left to my own company until evening. And
every evening you speak with me a little, but then you
send me to bed before you. What am I to think but
that you dislike my company? That you found my appearance distressing, my conversation irksome, and
my person of very little interest to you."

He tried a jest. "Your person of little interest? Nonsense! Does it truly seem that way when I come to
you at night?"

She went pale now but her voice was steady as she said, "Perhaps not. But you always say you do not mean to disturb me and it is I who find myself the forward one. Perhaps you wish I would not do so? Perhaps you would truly prefer that I did not disturb you?"

Now it was James who was shaken. He found himself kneeling before his bride and taking her hands in his, kissing each one in turn.

"My dearest Juliet," he said, "I had no notion you harbored such fears! We shall go away, I promise. Tomorrow. To the coast. There are things I shall need to do there but I promise I shall have more time to spend with you."

Her expression had softened as he spoke. But these last words caused her to snatch her hands out of his and rise to her feet. Indeed, she put some distance between them before she grasped the back of a chair, as though to give herself support before she confronted him.

"I see. What sorts of things? And how long do you expect we shall be there?"

James could not meet her eyes. He was in for it now and there was little or nothing to be done about it. He tried for an air of carelessness, "Oh, I don't know. A week or two. Perhaps a month. You will like the fresh, salt air. And I've some experiments to conduct."

"Some experiments?" Her voice held hope, even eagerness. "May I help you with them?"

Now he colored up. "No!" Then, as though aware that his hasty exclamation might sound too harsh, he added, "That is to say, you would only be bored."

Juliet took a step toward him, and now he could see there was a martial glint in her eyes. "No, I shouldn't," she countered.

"It will be at night," he added, taking a step back.

Juliet continued to advance. "I don't care," she said, clenching her teeth.

"It wouldn't be proper!" he replied, a hint of desperation in his voice.

"Proper?" Her voice came out as a squawk of protest. "Proper? Was it proper when you showed me the engine and we spent the night together? You did not seem to care so greatly for propriety then! Are you regretting the match we were forced into?"

Visibly shaken, he took a step toward her and held out his hand. "No! Of course not, Juliet!"

"Then why?" she demanded fiercely. "Why will you not let me be a part of this?"

"I cannot."

"But why? Have you taken me in distaste already?"

This time the desperation was in her voice and he swiftly closed the gap between them. James drew Juliet into his arms and held her close against his breast. His voice was soothing, his hand gentle as he stroked her hair and tried to answer his bride.

"Shhh, Juliet. It is not that, I swear! I am glad I married you! But I cannot let you help with this. It is not only my project. I cannot put you at any risk."

"Risk?"

Juliet echoed the word even as she pushed herself free. "What risk?"

There was alarm in her voice and now she was the one who looked very pale. James blanched and tried to repair the damage. He only made matters worse.

"Did I say risk? I only meant," he said, thinking quickly, "that is, we shall be at the coast. I, that is, there are smugglers, they say, along the coast. One or more may take exception if I am in their way or inadvertently cause them to have to alter their plans."

Her reaction was not what he had expected. With a fierceness that surprised both of them, Juliet said, "I shan't let you do it, then! Try your experiments somewhere else! I shan't let you put yourself at risk!"

But this was too much for James. He drew himself to his full height and said in a voice that would brook no opposition, "Juliet, you are my wife. You have no right to try to tell me what I may and may not do."

He was right. Juliet knew it only too well. It was the sort of thing she had been told all her life. But still she rebelled. Inwardly she might shudder at what her mother would say if she overheard this conversation but outwardly she stood her ground.

"I don't care," she said with a sniff. "You are my husband and your welfare is my concern. I don't want you to put yourself at risk!"

And then he understood that she truly cared. He drew in a deep breath and said, in the gentlest voice Juliet had ever heard, "Tomorrow we leave for the coast. And I shall do these experiments. I cannot explain, but it is a matter of honor and duty. I have given my word and I must keep it. And even if I had not, there are lives at stake. I cannot turn my back on them."

Juliet wanted to continue to defy him but she could not. Not when he spoke of duty and honor and saving lives. And yet she could not trust herself to speak. Instead she nodded. Finally she was able to command her voice enough to ask, "What time do we leave?"

"Nine o'clock in the morning."

Juliet nodded again. And then, because it still hurt that he would not confide in her, she turned on her heel and left the room.

James was very much mistaken if he thought the discussion over. He was about, she vowed, to discover just how stubborn his bride could be when she chose. One way or another she would persuade him to include her in his plans.

But Juliet had no chance to try. Though she lay awake almost until dawn, he never came to join her in the bed. And if her pillow was still damp with tears when Margaret came to wake her, both of them pretended not to notice.

Chapter 15

James stared out the window of their traveling coach. His mood was as gloomy as his expression. The situation was absurd! It still rankled that Juliet had ripped up at him the night before. And refused to speak to him over breakfast. Now she sat as far away from him as possible in the carriage and pretended that the dreary rain was of more interest than he was.

Didn't she understand how important this all was? And that there were some things a man simply could not tell his wife? Didn't she understand that he would have much preferred to have come to her last night than stay up and work as he had had to do?

James had the most bizarre impulse to reach over and pull Juliet onto his lap. And then to kiss her until her stiff posture gave way to the clinging embrace to which he had become accustomed of late.

But he did nothing of the sort. George said he must begin as he meant to go on. That Juliet must understand that he was her husband and she, as his wife, was obliged to follow his wishes. Still, he tried to coax her out of the sullens.

"Are you feeling unwell?" he asked.

"Unwell?" she echoed warily.

"Yes, unwell. I believe that traveling in a carriage

is often unsettling. My brother's wife is always subject to the megrims when they travel."

She stiffened and looked away, then back again. "It is not the weather which has given me the megrims," she said. "It is your behavior."

Well, that was blunt speaking. James tried to understand her. He truly did. But a man had only a certain amount of patience.

"Dash it all, this is absurd!" he said aloud. "I feel very much as though I were in my workshop handling volatile substances. One false step and there could be very unfortunate consequences. But at least if I were there, I should know what to expect. With women, with you, there is no knowing, no predicting, what might possibly occur. And that makes this all feel far more dangerous than any experiment in which I have yet engaged."

She gaped at him and then she laughed. He ought to have been offended, but instead James found himself laughing with her. And he reached out. She came into his arms willingly and let him pull her close against his chest.

In a tiny voice she said, "Please will you not let me help with whatever you plan to do?"

James sighed. "I wish that I could," he said, his voice as stern as he could make it. "But I was not joking or exaggerating when I said there might be danger. And I will not put you at risk."

Instantly she pulled away and moved to the opposite side of the carriage. She crossed her arms over her chest. She glared at him. It was the tear trickling down her cheek, and the surreptitious way she tried to wipe it away, that decided James. He also changed seats so that he was right next to her and he took her hand in his.

"My dear, please do not be unhappy," he said. "I want us to enjoy our time at the coast. I shall not always be working on my experiments. There shall be plenty of time for us to walk along the strand and do all manner of things together. Perhaps even talk. We have done scarcely enough of that since we were married."

Juliet looked at him then and there was hope, albeit tinged with wariness, in her eyes. James felt himself wanting to say or do something more that would please her.

He raised her gloved hand to his lips and pressed a fervent kiss on the palm. "We have not had much of a honeymoon, thus far," he told her, "but I swear that shall all change once we reach the coast."

And then he put an arm around Juliet and she allowed him to draw her head against his shoulder. To be sure, the top of her bonnet chafed his chin, but he was not about to cavil at such a minor detail. Not when she was once again in such a complaisant mood.

It was something of a surprise to James, the strength of the desire he felt in his breast to protect her and to make her happy. But it was not an altogether unpleasant sensation. He liked the notion, he discovered, of taking care of her. If, he thought sourly, she would only let him!

The Cock and Bull Inn was the most elegant establishment in the seaside town of Folkestone. This was not saying a great deal. Still, the proprietor of the Cock and Bull promised to do his best to make them happy.

"I'll have me missus kill and cook our plumpest chicken in your honor," he promised.

"Er, how kind of you," James said.

"Aye, well, now, there's not many Quality as stops here," the proprietor explained. "Mostly they goes to Dover. It's special like for us to have you here."

He seemed to wait expectantly for an explanation and James found himself blushing as he said, "Well, you see, it is our honeymoon and we don't precisely wish to encounter anyone we know, as we might in Dover."

"Aye, I can understand, sir," the proprietor said with a wink.

The man even kept an impassive expression when James explained that he tended to be restless at night and often went for walks and that would not present a problem, would it, when he returned?

As though scenting a handsome vail, the proprietor solemnly assured James that nothing he required would be a problem for the Cock and Bull. And then he had his eldest daughter show Juliet up to the inn's finest room.

"For I know you will be wishing to rest after your journey," the proprietor told her with an air of wanting to be of service.

Juliet did not object. She was tired and her nerves seemed stretched to the point that she did not know how she would get through the rest of the day.

To be sure, James had been all that was kind, and even affectionate, in the carriage. But he still meant to go out on his own, to do his experiments without her. And that was something she could not bear nor, she silently vowed as she followed the girl upstairs, was it something she meant to allow.

James was about to discover that he ought not to underestimate the woman he had married. And once he found out how useful she could be, surely he would forgive her completely what she meant to do.

So as they climbed the stairs, Juliet began to engage the girl ahead of her in quiet conversation. By the time she had been shown to the room, her bonnet removed, and a basin of water brought, she and the girl were in a fair way to making friends with one another. At the very least, they had reached an understanding.

An understanding of which she was certain James would not approve. But then, by the time he knew, it would be much too late for him to do anything about it. How fortunate it was, Juliet thought with a smug smile, that the coach carrying Margaret and the rest of the luggage had not yet arrived. For Margaret, as much as James, would have tried to stop her if she had been there.

By the time Margaret and the baggage arrived, with word that James was waiting for her in the private parlor below, Juliet was ready. She was wearing one of the gowns Mrs. Wise had made her, this one in her favorite shade of green, and it gave her a confidence she sorely needed.

James looked at her, a question in his eyes, when she came into the room. She smiled at him, albeit a trifle tremulously, and came forward to take the hand he held out to her.

"I don't wish us to quarrel," he said, kissing her forehead.

"Nor do I," she answered, meeting his gaze squarely.

He drew her over to the table. "I have arranged for tea and some refreshments for us. It was a long and tiring journey and you ate scarcely a morsel on the way."

He held out a chair for her and Juliet let him seat her. Still, she did not reach for her plate or cup. Instead, her hands clasped tightly together in her lap, she said, "You are very kind to me, James."

In the act of taking his own seat, he paused, looking startled. "I am your husband!" he said. "Of course it is my duty, my responsibility to look after your welfare."

Well, if it was not quite the declaration of love that Juliet would have liked to hear, at least it reassured her that however he felt, James would always try to make things as pleasant as possible for her.

If it was less than she wished, it was more than many brides could expect to hear. Juliet forced herself to smile and thank him and then allow James to serve her a slice of ham and a cup of tea. She would need, she reflected, to have all her strength whenever James chose to go out, on his own, to do his experiments.

But somewhat to her surprise, James made no effort to evade Juliet's company the rest of the day. Indeed, he suggested she change into sturdy shoes or boots and accompany him on a long walk. She did so gladly.

If she thought it strange he headed straight for the shore, she did not say so. If she thought it strange he addressed scarcely a word to her on their excursion, she said not a word. If he muttered about angles and heights and light intensities, she said not a word.

Instead, she stored up every moment to consider carefully later. It was enough, for the moment, to be in his company, to be at his side. She would not distract him with idle chatter. He had once called her a sensible woman and said it as if it were the greatest compliment he could bestow. She would do her best to live up to that encomium.

It was dark when they returned to the inn, and to her delight, James came to bed with her. He made love to her with a tenderness that drew him even more deeply into her heart than before. And she knew that no matter what happened, she would never let go of this man. With a fierceness she had not known she possessed, Juliet vowed that for the rest of her life, she would be at his side.

James lay quiet in the darkness, his arms still around Juliet. He found himself wondering why he had waited so long to marry and whether Juliet could possibly be as happy with him as he found himself with her.

To be sure, he had not bargained on anything stronger than mutual respect when they wed. Indeed, he had come to think himself incapable of anything more. But somehow Juliet had found a way inside his heart and he found himself silently vowing to keep her there forever.

It was a very strange feeling, James thought, but a rather wonderful one as well. In the morning he would have to say something of the sort to Juliet. Although, perhaps, on second thought, he ought not to do so. After all, she had married him only because propriety dictated they marry. Perhaps she would be embarrassed by an effusive display of emotion.

For the first time in his life, James wished he had paid as much attention to the ladies as he had to his inventions. To be sure, no one could pay a compliment better than he or entertain a hostess with a more deliciously scandalous *on-dit*.

But when it came to actually courting a lady, James had never done so and he was not entirely certain how to begin now, with Juliet.

For now, however, he had a man to meet. Careful not to wake Juliet, he slipped out of bed and dressed quickly. But he waited to put his shoes on until he was outside the door.

Downstairs, in the public room, he found the place crowded. The innkeeper smiled at him in a knowing way, and to his annoyance, James felt himself flush.

"Need a brew, do you, to revive your, er, spirits?" the fellow asked with an impertinent wink.

James drew himself up to give the man a setdown, but before he could speak, someone appeared at his elbow. A rather shabbily dressed fellow who had obviously had too much to drink.

"Now, now, don't roast the poor feller," the new man said, slurring his words a bit. To James he added, "You must be the newlywed."

This time James really did intend to put an end to the impertinence. Right up until the moment he looked closely at the fellow's face. Then he could barely conceal his astonishment.

"No need to be ashamed," the man said, tapping the side of his nose. "Every man needs a tipple or two once he realizes just what he's gotten himself into, marriage-wise. Ask any married man here."

"I, er, that is—"

A drink was pressed into James's hands and he allowed the fellow to tug him over to a table in the corner. "Sit, sit," the man said amiably. "Let me tell you a tale or two about my second wife. Or was it my fourth?"

Several others in the room shook their heads at the man but lost interest as he mumbled some long-winded story that clearly had no point. Fascination as much as anything else kept James in his seat.

His patience was rewarded. When the other man was certain no one was paying them any attention, he leaned closer, as though to impart words of wisdom. And then suddenly his voice was no longer that of a country bumpkin but rather the cultured accents James had heard so recently in London.

"My apologies about the towers. I had assumed they were on a cliff, not down on the beach to repel invasion. Nor did I realize they would likely be inhabited."

James followed the other man's lead. He leaned forward, his chin on one hand, elbow on the table, as if the pint had gone to his head.

"What now?" he whispered back.

Frederick Baines roared with laughter as though James had just said something terribly funny. He seemed, James thought indignantly, to be greatly enjoying himself! What sort of man was he that he had no trouble pretending to be a drunken lout of a fellow?

Then Baines leaned forward again, his voice devoid of humor as he said, "We look around tomorrow, a bit farther afield, but if, as I fear, we find nothing suitable, then we'd best push on to Dover. I don't like having to be so close to the castle, but I can think of no place else likely to provide the setting you need. If all else fails us, there is a tower within the castle walls there that looks out to sea. With the letter your brother gave you, the governor will most certainly agree to let you use it. We shall meet again here tomorrow night, and if we still have not found any suitable spot around here, then we'll meet again in Dover, a day or two after that, all right?"

James nodded. It was, at least, something of a plan and he could think of none better.

"You'd best go now," Baines said. "We are starting to attract attention. Let it look as though you've finally had your fill of me."

It was, James discovered, something rather exciting to play a part. Was this what drew actors to the stage? He could begin to understand it as he felt the heady thrill of successfully deceiving the others in the public room. He even allowed himself to stagger slightly as he made his way toward the stairs.

Apparently this was a touch Baines thought excessive for his voice called out, "Quality! Can'ts hold their liquor worth a damn, can they?"

That hastened James's footsteps, and a few minutes later, he was safely upstairs in his room. Too late he realized he ought to have asked Baines which tower he was supposed to ask the governor of Dover Castle to allow him to use. A new tower? An old one? There could be any number of possibilities. The devil take it, why hadn't he thought to ask?

He could, he supposed, go back downstairs. But that would draw far too much attention to the both of them. No, time enough to find out tomorrow. If he were lucky, either he or Baines would find something right nearby Folkestone. If not, then it was off to Dover and Dover Castle to meet with the governor and discover what he could. After all, any suitable tower would do, would it not?

Thus uneasily reassured, James undressed and slipped back into bed. Time enough, he thought, to worry about all of this in the morning.

Chapter 16

Two mornings later, Juliet found herself thoroughly confused. James was as affectionate as she could have wished. She had not expected, to be sure, that anyone made love in the morning. But she could not help conceding it was a very pleasant notion. And he was as gentle as she had ever known him to be.

Then, abruptly, as he lay holding her afterward, James suddenly pulled free his arm and sat bolt upright. "We had best get up," he said briskly as he got out of bed. "I mean to move us to another place today."

Juliet blinked at him, too stunned, for a moment, to react. Then abruptly she sat up as well. "Why?" she demanded.

"Why what?" he asked cautiously.

"Why must we move? And why can we not do so later?"

"Oh, er, it is just that I do not like to lose the morning light. If we arrive at our new stopping place by noon, then we shall have time to go for a walk this afternoon."

He evaded her gaze. He colored bright red. He hastily turned away. All signs, Juliet thought with a grim expression, that something very strange was going on. Well, if he could pretend that it was not, then so could she!

With a briskness that matched his, Juliet climbed out of bed and began reaching for the basin of water. Then, in an act of pure mischief, she dropped her nightshift to the floor, leaving herself completely uncovered in front of James.

With her back toward him, Juliet could only guess at what he was thinking. But she did hear something that sounded suspiciously like his hairbrush hitting the floor. She bent forward to wash her face and thought she heard a moan. Even better. Then she turned around, and careful not to meet his eyes because she did not think she could keep her expression impassive if she did so, Juliet calmly sauntered the length of the room to where her clothes were hanging.

Without the least haste she chose everything she needed for the day. So far as she could tell, James stood stock-still behind her and she could not resist saying, "Come, James, shouldn't you hurry? You did say you wanted to leave as soon as possible."

He stammered some sort of reply that was incoherent to both of them. Then, abruptly, he began to move around the room, swiftly gathering up what he needed. By the time Juliet had donned her most intimate garments, including her chemise, she turned to find James fully dressed and headed toward the doorway.

"But James," she said, with an air of innocence as she pulled her gown over her head, "you cannot desert me now. I shall need your assistance to fasten up my dress."

He gulped. He visibly gulped. "I shall send your maid up to you," he said, reaching for the door handle.

"But James," she said, a hint of petulance in her voice, "I should like you to help me."

He closed his eyes and sighed and then opened them again. Gingerly he approached. Juliet turned her back to him and lifted her hair up and out of the way. Were his hands trembling as he did up the fastenings?

It certainly felt so but she dared not try to look. She was, after all, pretending to be oblivious to his reactions.

And then he was done and heading for the door faster than before. "Wait, James!" she said again. "I am ready to go with you."

Above all else he was a gentleman. There was nothing for James to do but to wait for her and even offer Juliet his arm when she reached his side. Without a word, but with the sunniest smile in the world, she took it. And together they went down to the private parlor for breakfast.

What the devil was he going to do? James wondered. It was bad enough when he reacted to Juliet this way under the covers at night. Every night. Or even in the morning. But it was most unseemly to do so out of bed and in daylight!

If it did not stop, then surely, sooner or later, she would notice. James shuddered to think what her reaction would be when she did. Juliet was a gently bred young lady. She had a right to expect him to treat her with respect. Not as if she was some strumpet who existed solely for his pleasure.

She could not possibly realize the effect she had on him. And she would be most embarrassed if she ever did. It was clearly his duty to protect her from such knowledge. But how was he to do so when she persisted in behaving in such a way around him?

It was proof of her innocence, of course. Had she the slightest notion—but she could not, he had already established that to his own satisfaction. Still, he must do something to warn her away from such behavior as this morning when she was dressing. Daresay it came from being around only females. One wouldn't need so much modesty in front of other females. If one was female oneself.

Bewildered, James wondered just how he was going

to bring his naive bride to a clear sense of what she was doing without distressing her any more than was absolutely necessary.

Fortunately the need to deal with that dilemma was suddenly overshadowed when James had to arrange for their departure. The proprietor of the Cock and Bull was offended. Grievously offended.

"Your valet said you meant to stay at least two weeks," he said, with a disdainful sniff.

"My valet was mistaken. Besides, I've changed m'mind," James replied gamely.

"I have already been paid in advance for the days and laid out much of it in anticipation of the meals you would require and an extra servant for the establishment during your stay," the proprietor countered.

"Keep the funds!" James said, a hint of desperation in his voice.

"The insult to my establishment! The entire countryside will know," the proprietor persisted.

"M'wife. She's subject to megrims. Needs a different view," James said, unable to think of anything else.

Juliet opened her mouth to protest, and without the slightest hesitation, he tromped on her foot under the table. She glared at him, but she pressed her lips together and did not speak.

"You may tell everyone how eccentric my wife is," James offered. "Everyone will surely understand that. Women are notorious for their whims and whimsy."

The proprietor nodded slowly. "True," he agreed grudgingly. "Me own wife takes fire at the least little thing. Nothing that anyone sensible could possibly find objectionable. Very well, sir. I cannot say I like it, but when do you wish your carriage to be ready for your departure?"

"Oh, in an hour," James said carelessly. "I daresay it will take that long for m'wife's maid and my man to pack up our things anyway. Will you tell them to get started at once?"

"Yes, sir."

This last was said with something of a malicious air and James guessed that things were not going altogether smoothly below stairs. Still, soon they would be on their way and none of it would matter.

He was just congratulating himself on how smoothly he had handled things when Juliet looked at him across the table and said, in an unnaturally even voice that alarmed him, "If you must make up farradiddles, I do wish you would leave me out of them."

James spread his hands. "But there was nothing else he would accept as a reason."

She nodded. And just as he was about to give a sigh of relief, she said, "Yes, you convinced him. But how are you going to convince me that this move is necessary?"

He stared at her in disbelief. "But . . . but you are my wife. I don't need to explain anything to you."

With a sinking sensation, James realized that Juliet was now staring at him with equal disbelief. She spoke slowly, as though keeping her temper barely in check.

"You don't need to explain to me? Because I am your wife? I suppose you are saying that I must do whatever you wish, whenever you wish, merely because you are a man?"

"No," James said, eager to correct her error, "you must do it because you are my wife."

"I see."

Juliet rose slowly to her feet and James felt a distinct sensation of alarm. Before he could find out, however, what she intended, the door to the private parlor opened and a servant brought in a tray of food.

"Here now, the missus has made a very nice collation for you," the woman said, bustling about, setting out plates and food. "You'll find yourself nicely filled after eating all this, I'll be bound!"

"I shall be surprised if we manage to eat the half of it!" Juliet told the woman, with a merry smile.

The woman smiled back and winked at Juliet. "Well, a new bride as you are, and your husband new at this as well, the missus was thinking you'd be wanting and needing to keep up your strength."

Juliet blushed, becomingly in James's opinion, but she did not take offense. James felt himself blush when the woman had the temerity to wink at him. But he could think of no seemly way to reprove her without acknowledging the implications behind the wink.

Still, he felt greatly relieved when the woman said, "I'll be bound you don't need me around. You'll want to be alone, you will. I'll be back later to collect the dishes. Enjoy your breakfast now!"

The moment the door closed behind the woman, James and Juliet looked at one another and burst out laughing.

He could only feel relief that her anger was apparently forgotten. Before he could enjoy the feeling, however, his bride rose to her feet and said, primly, "I had best go upstairs and help Margaret pack."

"But wait! You haven't eaten!" he protested.

She smiled without humor or amiability and indeed curtseyed before she said, "Consider that one more of my whims, sir."

And then she was gone. James started to follow but then decided that perhaps it would be wiser, after all, to give her some time to herself. Besides, someone ought to eat the breakfast the cook had provided. Especially if he was going to spend the afternoon tramping about the cliffs at Dover.

Let Juliet have her whims and megrims. He was the husband. It was for her to come to him and apologize, scarcely the other way around.

By the time he had finished eating, James had even halfway convinced himself that something of the sort might actually happen. He was almost whistling as he entered the bedchamber he and Juliet shared. And halted in the doorway, his mouth gaping open. Juliet stood there holding a mirror, one that he recognized only too well as his father's, and she had one piece of it in each hand.

The look of dismay on her face matched his own, and even though he had never liked that mirror, James felt something tug at his heart at the thought it was broken.

"I was trying to help pack," she said.

But he scarcely heard her. Instead he took several steps forward, noticing that both Woods and her maid were as far away as possible from the pair of them. He held out his hands and she put the two pieces of the mirror into them.

"I think it was meant to come apart," she said, a catch in her voice.

This time he heard her. Wanted to hear her. "Meant to come apart?" he echoed.

"There seems to be something inside."

James walked past her, carrying the two pieces of the intricately embossed mirror, and sat on the edge of the bed. He tried to take in what she had just said. Carefully, very carefully, he set one piece of the mirror on the bed and looked at the other.

It was true that it didn't seem to be broken. The edges were smooth and there was something resembling a catch. And a piece of paper folded several times and tucked into those same edges.

Even more carefully James removed and unfolded the paper, the second part to the mirror set beside the first on the bed where it could not slip to the floor by accident.

The first glance told him the letter was in French. A second that it was beyond his level of understanding of the language. His mind had run more to math and science and his tutor had early on despaired of teaching James more than the rudiments of any language other than English.

But Juliet could read it. Without his noticing, she had come to sit beside him and look at the paper too. Now James realized she was silently mouthing the words as she translated them to herself.

"What does it say?" he asked curtly.

She looked at him, dismay in her clear, green eyes. Her hands, he noticed, were clasped tightly together. James could not begin to guess at the cause of her distress. So he did everything he could think of to set her at ease. He fitted the pieces of the mirror back together and curtly told Woods and Juliet's maid to finish packing. Then he took the letter in one hand and grasped her arm with the other.

"Come, let us wait in the private parlor," he told Juliet. "They will tell us when it is time to go."

She was pale, very pale, but she came. Once they were in the private parlor she began to pace, her distraction clear even to his eyes.

"What does the paper say?" James asked again.

"You do not know?" she asked.

When he shook his head, there seemed to be some relief in her expression, a slight easing to the tension with which she held herself.

Quietly he said, "I do not know French very well. I was the despair of my tutor, in that respect. Come, what does it say?" When she still did not answer, he added, "That was my father's mirror. His dressing case, I inherited after he died. We divided up his possessions so that each of us had something. It was commissioned for him, or so I have always been told. Which means the paper must have been his. I beg of you to tell me what it says."

She turned then and met his eyes, searching for something. At last she seemed to make up her mind. She took a deep breath, nodded to herself, and then she spoke.

"You have said your father was a notable reformer. Did he, perhaps, admire the principles of the French revolution?" she asked.

"Yes, but not the excesses!" James replied with a frown, remembering. "He said it was an experiment sadly gone awry."

"Would he have been sympathetic to Monsieur Bonaparte?"

"No! Absolutely not!"

"Are you quite certain?" Juliet asked, coming to stand beside James and put a hand on his shoulder. "Or is that what you wish to believe."

James shook off her hand and rose to his feet. This time it was he who paced the room. "My father would never have betrayed England. That is what you are suggesting, are you not? He wanted change, but not change that overturned everything as they did in France!"

"Then why," she asked, her voice heartbreakingly gentle, "did he have a letter from Monsieur Bonaparte saying that he counts on his support?"

James went very pale and sank into the nearest chair. He looked again at the letter he still clutched in his hand. "There is no name at the top," he said. "We cannot be certain it was directed to my father."

She turned and looked out the window, as though afraid to let him see her face. Over her shoulder she said, "There would not be, if Monsieur Bonaparte was discreet."

James took several deep breaths. Finally he stood and said, in a deadly calm voice, "It is understandable that you would think what you do. But I know my father. As young as I was when he died, I am still certain he would never, never have aided the French. Or supported Napoleon Bonaparte. It would have gone against everything he believed in to do so, reformer or not."

And then, because he could not trust himself a moment longer with someone who believed his father could have been a traitor, James started to leave the room.

"Where are you going?" she asked.

He paused, his hand on the door, to say, "To put this back where it was. Until we know the truth of the matter, the fewer people who see it the better."

"Why not just burn the letter?" Juliet asked. "Then no one need see it ever again."

"We Langfords do not run from the truth. No matter how unpleasant it may be. My father kept this letter for a reason. Until I know what that reason may have been, I cannot destroy it."

Then, before she could ask any more questions, he was gone.

Chapter 17

Dover was bustling but Woods managed to engage a suite of rooms for James and Juliet.

"It is not perhaps entirely what you are accustomed to, sir," Woods explained, "but I thought you would be more comfortable a little out of the way of the busiest part of town. I have engaged a private parlor, of course, as well as bedchambers and stabling for the horses and carriage."

"Excellent!" James said approvingly.

Woods turned to Juliet. "I believe you will be pleased to find that you need not walk past the public taproom every time you enter or leave the building."

The establishment was, she was relieved to see, quite respectable and Woods was correct in saying that it would suit them very well. She went upstairs alone. Her understanding, with the innkeeper's daughter in Folkestone, might have come to nothing, but she would, she thought grimly, try again here.

"Er, I think I shall go for a walk," James came to tell her, a short time later.

"I shall go with you," Juliet immediately countered. "It is a beautiful day and I should enjoy that very much."

He did not look entirely pleased, but Juliet refused to be discouraged. If this marriage was to work, she must enter into his interests. Besides, she wanted to discover what he intended.

So they walked. James tried to be a pleasant companion, but it was evident he was distracted.

"The cliffs are too blasted open," he muttered. "Everything can be seen from the town and from the castle!"

"Yes, but what should that matter?" Juliet asked.

"Er, never mind," he hastily replied.

"One can see a great distance," she said helpfully.

"Too far."

"Is there somewhere in particular you wish to walk?" she asked at last, when they had been going in what seemed like circles for more than an hour.

"What? Er, no. That is, perhaps we ought to return to the inn," he said gruffly.

And then, as though he realized she might be feeling a trifle neglected, James slipped his arm around Juliet's waist and he was once again her own dear husband.

Hours later, well after midnight, men moved through the dark streets of Dover. They carried barrels and boxes and something more.

A few caskets of French brandy were deposited in the usual place, by the back door of each inn where arrangements had been made in advance. And then the men moved on and no one, save for the proprietors who had been listening for them, even knew they had come and gone.

" 'Ere now," one said. "Not so much noise."

"The moon's too bright," another grumbled. "We'll be seen for sure."

"Not if we does our job and gets out of 'ere right quick," still a third replied. "Just keeps a sharp eye out for the king's guard."

And then they moved on. Above their heads, James and Juliet slept soundly. Only Frederick Baines, in another part of town, noted and worried over their presence when they passed by his lodgings.

The next morning Juliet smiled brightly at James over breakfast. "What shall we do today?" she asked.

He noted her smile with a sinking sensation in the pit of his stomach. "We? Er, that is, I must visit the castle this morning," he told her with unaccustomed diffidence. "But I think perhaps it would be best if you stayed here in town. After I return, perhaps we could walk down to the harbor and look at the ships at dock there."

She regarded him over the rim of her cup and frowned. "You do not wish me to go with you to the castle? You are ashamed to take me with you?"

There was hurt in Juliet's voice and James made haste to reassure her. "No, no, of course that is not what I meant. It is just that the castle is now a military facility."

"Then why are you going to visit there?" she asked with a shrewdness that was most alarming.

James developed an intense interest in the food on his plate before he answered her.

"I, er, that is the governor is an old friend of my father. I ought to pay my respects," he improvised.

Even without looking at Juliet, he knew that her eyes were narrowed in the way he had come to associate with an argument about to take place. She was, he just knew she was, going to insist on coming along with him. He was right.

"Perhaps I ought to pay my respects as well," she said.

"No, no, it is not necessary, I assure you."

There was a hint of steel in her voice as she said, "I think it is."

"Perhaps," he said, with a patently false smile and a hint of desperation in his voice, "you could visit the

church there while I am speaking to the governor.
That might be unexceptionable."

To his surprise she brightened at the suggestion. So
much so that James felt a distinct sense of alarm. But
it was too late to withdraw the invitation. He could
only hope that the guards would deny her entrance to
the castle grounds.

He was not so fortunate.

Meanwhile, Frederick Baines was well ahead of
James and Juliet. Even as they argued in the private
parlor of their inn, he surveyed the old Roman tower
thoughtfully. It was indeed as he remembered it to be.
It would do. To be sure, he could not like the notion
of these experiments being carried out so close to
where French prisoners of war were housed, but there
was no choice.

Did men still think it haunted, he wondered? If not,
lights, a sheet blowing in the moonlight, which they
would need anyway to hide from the castle side what
they were doing, these should reinforce whatever notions remained about ghosts and such in the tower and
keep the curious away.

Baines nodded to himself, then turned into the
church. This was the only possible tower they could
use. The governor would have to give permission to
James to do his experiments here. He must. Baines
knew only too well how persuasive the document was
that his young friend carried. After all, he had helped
Sir Thomas Levenger to craft it in London. Now it was
time, indeed past time, for him to play his own role.

Strictly speaking, he ought to have been presenting
himself for duty to someone else first, but under the
circumstances, Frederick preferred to go unnoticed by
anyone other than the chaplain for as long as possible.
His papers, created by himself, would not pass inspec-
tion if anyone thought to check with the person who
was supposed to have signed them.

The chaplain was inside the church arranging the cloth at the altar. Baines cleared his throat to let the fellow know he was there.

"Yes? Yes?" the chaplain asked querulously.

The fellow was elderly. Good. That meant he was all the more likely to welcome Baines's arrival and his offer of assistance.

Frederick drew out the letter, written only last night, which carried a seal he ought not to have been able to counterfeit. With a diffidence no one who knew him socially would have recognized, he said, "I'm to be your new assistant, sir."

The chaplain all but snatched the letter out of Frederick's hand, so eager was he to read it.

"An assistant? They've sent me an assistant? But why, after all this time?" the chaplain demanded suspiciously. "They've never sent me one before."

Baines let himself sigh and look down at the ground. "It is," he said with what seemed to be a great reluctance, "my penance to be here. The bishop himself arranged everything. He said it was worth any amount of trouble to him to have me so far out of the way."

"Why?" the chaplain asked with pardonable suspicion.

Frederick Baines sighed again. "I like towers," he said. "I am forever climbing up in them and ringing the bells. The bishop thought I ought to be busy within the church and the pulpit instead. But you see," he said, spreading his hands in a patent plea for understanding, "I do not like to preach. Nor to be surrounded by people. I prefer towers. So he banished me here. I think he knows the governor," he added with just the right note of gloominess in his voice.

The chaplain allowed himself, for the briefest of moments, to dwell on the kindness of providence that had sent him such a man. He wanted to grin from relief or to leap into the air with joy that he need never go into the tower again. The chaplain even felt the temptation to clap his hands with delight. But he did not.

Such a display would have been unseemly and so, instead, the chaplain put on his most fatherly expression and patted his new assistant on the shoulder.

In a soothing voice he said, "Do not worry. I shall not make you take the pulpit. And I shall even allow you, since it is what you wish, to take over all duties with regard to the bell tower."

Frederick, in his guise as assistant, gave thanks in suitable terms, and in amicable accord the chaplain began to show him about the church.

He ought not, the chaplain told himself, to be so very happy. He ought long ago to have conquered his fear of the ghosts who were said to haunt the tower. But for this moment, the chaplain decided, he would allow himself to be human enough to feel profound gratitude and relief for the new man's arrival.

An hour or two later, the governor of Dover Castle regarded his own assistant with a distinct lack of pleasure. "We've got what?"

"A London gentleman, sir, insisting on seeing you," the soldier replied, carefully keeping his eyes on a point well beyond the governor's right shoulder. "Brought his wife, apparently. She's out looking at the church, I'm told. But he insists on speaking with you, personally, sir."

"Blast and confound it! Very well, I suppose I must see him, but mind, I'll give him short shrift and you may tell him so as you bring him in."

"Yes, sir."

But the London gentleman did not seem in the least discomposed by the warning. Indeed, he seemed entirely at ease. Not even the presence of a French prisoner of war in the antechamber appeared to give him pause. But then perhaps he didn't realize that was who the scruffy creature was.

Nor did he speak until the door had closed behind him and he was alone with the governor of Dover Castle. And even then it was the governor who spoke first.

"What the devil brings you here, sir? I'll have you know this is a military installation and we've prisoners of war on the grounds. It is not a place for idle sightseers. I cannot understand why you were admitted at all but you were and so it's my duty to tell you that I'll thank you to take yourself—and your wife—off elsewhere!"

In reply the London gentleman merely drew a set of papers from a pocket of his coat and handed them to the governor. In a voice that was mild to the point of diffidence he said, "These are the reason I was admitted. I think you will find these in order."

The governor gave him a sharp glance and an even sharper one after he had a chance to look through the papers. "What the devil?" he asked again, but this time softly.

The gentleman took back the papers and bowed. "A simple request, sir. Have you any towers hereabouts?"

"Towers, Mr. Langford?" the governor gaped. "What sort of towers?"

James Langford frowned. Once again he regretted not asking for more details from Frederick Baines.

"I'm not quite certain," he allowed. "Any sorts of towers. Perhaps even an unfinished tower."

Indignation flashed in the governor's eyes. "Sir, had I received orders to build a tower, I had it built. Completely. And if you mean the Martello towers, as I presume you do, then you must know that I cannot allow a civilian near any one of them."

Langford hastily raised his hands. "I meant no slander, sir. It's just, well, I need access to a tower and I was told there was one I might be able to use here. I need one that is particularly tall, you see."

The governor hesitated. It went against the grain to help this dandy. But in the end he said begrudgingly, "There is a tower. A bell tower. Next to the church, within the castle walls. It was originally Roman I'm told and built onto, some time ago. It is perhaps twelve meters high."

"Perfect! I wonder if you could arrange that no patrols pass near it? Indeed, it would be best if your patrols took no notice of me whatsoever, wherever they might see me. Particularly at night? That even the chaplain of the church stays away?"

Now the governor gaped at his visitor. He would have protested but the papers were clear. This man was to be given any assistance he asked for. Finally he closed his mouth, drew a deep breath through his nose, and then said, "Very well, Mr. Langford. I shall direct that there be no patrols near the tower. And they are to ignore you whenever they see you. But I make no promises for the chaplain. It is up to you to persuade him."

James Langford nodded.

"For how long do you mean to be here, using this tower?" the governor could not keep from asking.

"Until you hear otherwise."

It went against the grain but the governor made himself nod his head. He took a malicious satisfaction in knowing the chaplain would be no more pleased at the request than he was himself and might even refuse to agree. It was, after all, the church bell tower.

But Langford seemed to have no inkling of any possible trouble. He bowed. "Thank you. Then I shall take up no more of your time, sir."

The governor rose to his feet and watched him leave. A moment later his aide de camp entered the room. "Sir?" the younger man asked.

"We are to withdraw all patrols from the area near the bell tower. We are to appear to notice nothing that goes on there," the governor said, avoiding his aide's fascinated gaze. "Apparently our visitor has an interest in such things and does not wish to be disturbed. He plans to come and go, it seems, at night and our patrols are to ignore him. No matter what they see."

"But sir, that would be unwise. Doesn't he know about the smugglers hereabouts?"

The governor smiled and it was not a pretty smile. "London allows one of society's most notorious gamesters and wastrels to give me orders and I am to warn him? A Langford? A son of the late Lord Darton? No, I think not. If something did happen to the fellow, I assure you no one would be worse off for it. He would tell me nothing so I shall tell him nothing. Now, where is that troublemaking prisoner? We'll deal with him, once and for all!"

Chapter 18

James found Juliet in the church where he had left her. The chaplain was showing her about and talking about the history of the church and castle. He breathed a sigh of relief that she seemed content and had stayed where she was supposed to stay.

"I wonder if we might trouble you to show us the bell tower," James said to the chaplain, shortly after he had joined them.

The chaplain hesitated. He fluttered his hands. "I really don't think you wish to go in there," he said. "But if you insist, then perhaps my assistant could show you about. He should be around here somewhere."

In a bored, well-bred voice, James said, "Yes, I suppose that would be acceptable."

"Good, good. I am sure you will find him at the tower itself. He seems to have a fondness for towers, you see."

James bowed and escorted his wife out of the church. The assistant had a fondness for the tower? That could prove a problem, he thought. He wondered what Baines was going to say when he found out.

Beside him, Juliet stirred restlessly and James made himself speak to her, almost at random. But his mind was focused on the tower. It was right where the governor had said it would be, next to the church and the closest point, save for the castle walls, to the top of the cliffs. Perfect for his purpose. If the assistant could be dealt with, that is.

They came upon the assistant almost at once. He was moving about the base of the tower, talking absentmindedly to himself. James was rather taken aback until he recognized who the fellow was. It was very fortunate, he thought grimly, that Juliet had never met the man before so that she could not do so.

The man stopped as he noticed them. He waved a hand at the tower. "Yes, yes, polish 'er up, the bells. A nice tower, too. Tall she be."

James felt the greatest urge to laugh. He was, for a moment, too stunned by this display to even speak. But Juliet was not.

"Er, excuse me?" she said brightly, as though determined to pretend not to have noticed the fellow's eccentricity. "Could we please see the tower? The chaplain said you would show us about."

The fellow hesitated. He looked at Juliet and then he looked at James. Finally he nodded and opened the door for them into the tower.

"I've an interest in astronomy," James said in an offhand manner as they climbed upward toward the bells. "I don't suppose I might be allowed to bring my telescope here some night?"

The man rubbed his chin. "I s'pose it wouldn't hurt none. A telescope, you say?"

"Yes. My device for seeing the stars better."

"Hmmm, I've a fancy to see that for myself. If you tell me when you might like to do it, I'll meet you here and help you with the contraption."

"Thank you," James replied. He paused then added, even more carelessly than before, "Does anyone else, hereabouts, wonder about this tower? Anyone more curious than they ought to be?"

The fellow snorted. "Not likely. Aside from it's the

bell tower for the church, no one wants nothing to do with the place now what they all know it's haunted."

"Haunted?" Juliet asked, a hint of fear in her voice.

James started to explain that there were no such things as ghosts when it occurred to him that it might be useful if she believed there were. So instead he patted her arm and said, soothingly, "Not during the day, I believe."

The man nodded. "That's right, ma'am. Nighttime, that's when you want to worry."

Juliet shivered. She distinctly shivered and James put a consoling arm about her. "Never fear," he said, "I shall make certain nothing happens to you."

She glared at him but did not pull away. Their new friend nodded helpfully. "Aye, that's the ticket, ma'am. You let your man here keep you safe. You don't want to be mucking about this 'ere tower anyways. Not with ghosts of Romans hanging about."

Juliet stared at the man climbing ahead of her and shivered again. It was not precisely that she actually believed him when he said the tower was haunted. After all, how could it be, dedicated to the church as it was, and yet there was something about it she intensely disliked.

Still, she would not say so aloud. Nor regret her foolishness, not if it inclined James to put his arm around her waist. That was, after all, a remarkably nice feeling. To know that he wished to reassure her.

And she could see the wariness of the man before her melt away as he was now able to dismiss her as a foolish female. Her thoughts strayed to the clothing her mother had insisted she bring with her when she married. The dresses with frills and furbelows she had thus far refused to allow her maid to lay out for her. Perhaps that had been a mistake.

Certainly when she had gone about dressed as her mother wished, others were far more inclined to underestimate Juliet. And her intelligence. Then it had enraged her but now, well, now she could begin to see the advantages of such a thing.

Lost in thought, Juliet almost missed the look that passed between her husband and the other man. Almost. So they had secrets, did they? Well, she had secrets too. She said not a word as they talked with one another. Instead she allowed herself the luxury of pressing close to James and feeling his arm tightening in a comforting way about her waist.

And when they were done and James led her away from the tower, she did not object. No, nor did she do so when he found a place to sit and pulled her onto his lap. She simply tucked her hand into his and allowed him to stroke her back reassuringly as he murmured comforting words into her ears.

"I did not mean to distress you," he said. "I had no notion the tower was haunted."

Juliet snuggled closer.

"There truly is no danger during the day," he added.

She nodded.

"But if you like, we could go back to the inn now."

"I should like that," she agreed meekly.

He set her on her feet and they started walking toward the castle walls. Only when they were outside and halfway back to the town did she say, "I don't recall a telescope among the baggage we packed."

He colored up and avoided meeting her eyes. "I, er, it is with the luggage. It is still strapped to the traveling coach."

"I see. May I come with you when you bring it to the tower?"

"No! That is, it will be dark and I do not like the notion of you out of doors so late and in such a place as this," he said, all but stumbling over the words.

Juliet had to bite back an angry reply. It would be the argument in London all over again if she did not.

So instead of saying the things she wished to say, Juliet smiled a small, tight smile and nodded. On the surface it seemed she was all amiability. But underneath she was making her own plans for the evening.

Juliet dressed in her frilliest frock for dinner and then dismissed Margaret for the rest of the night. She let the maid draw her own, incorrect conclusions as to what that meant. As for the dress, it had precisely the effect she hoped it would have on James's estimate of her intelligence. After dinner she went upstairs ahead of him. He came to visit her, tucked up into bed, and kiss her on the forehead as he promised not to be out too late.

The moment he was gone, Juliet slipped from under the covers and pulled the nightgown over her head. How fortunate that its voluminous folds hid so well the shirt and breeches she had begged from the maid who worked at the inn. She also reached for her spectacles. She could not afford to trip over anything in the dark, and that was likely enough during the day if she did not wear them.

As arranged, the girl was waiting for her on the back stairs. "Here's the dagger you wished for, ma'am," the girl said, handing over a wicked-looking thing.

Juliet tucked the knife into the boots she had also borrowed from the servant. "Thank you. I am not so foolish as to go out tonight without some means of protecting myself. Were you able to find a horse for me?"

The girl shook her head. "No, ma'am. But I found a donkey. Right reliable he'll be. He's tied out back now. I'll be pleased to show you."

"Yes, that will do," Juliet agreed.

It was amazing, she thought, just how useful it could be to cultivate the acquaintance of servants. In minutes she was on her way, careful to take a more circuitous route out of the town than James would.

It was also useful that she had memorized so thoroughly the route back from the tower. And the location of the small door in the castle walls that she was certain James intended to use to gain entrance.

Juliet reached the castle not far behind James. He had his valet in tow, and the man who had spoken with them that afternoon was waiting at the little castle door to help carry things inside. The carriage was apparently to wait. She kept her distance until they were done and then she tied the donkey to the back of the carriage and slipped through the doorway.

She moved silently toward the tower, hoping not to meet any patrols. It seemed absurd for James to set up his equipment here, inside the castle walls, but then he wasn't truly interested in astronomy. His talk of lights and lenses had given away that much! He might think she had forgotten their discussions in London, but she had not.

Juliet waited, hidden by the walls of the church, until she was certain the last trip had been made into the tower with James's equipment and then she quietly slipped up to the door. She listened and all was silent. Above her she could hear voices and she decided it was safe to slip inside.

Before she could do so, however, the door started to open and she had to hastily hide on the other side of the tower. She heard the valet come out, grumbling to himself about his employer's odd fits and starts. And the weight of the equipment he was expected to help carry. The man wandered some distance away and sat down with his back to the castle walls to wait.

Juliet had to wait until the man closed his eyes. Only when she heard the reassuring sound of snoring did she dare come out of her hiding place and slip inside the tower. One way or another, she was going to find out what was going on!

Above her were low voices.

"Fix the sheet so the light cannot be seen from the castle side."

"And how do you want the lantern set up?"

"Here. And now the lenses. Yes, that one first."

The voices dropped lower so Juliet could not hear what they were saying. Astronomy indeed! she thought with a snort of disgust.

Juliet slipped back outside the tower, where she would have a better view of what was going on. Flashes of light, then none, then the whole thing repeated over again. The experiment continued for some time and then it stopped abruptly.

She could hear the sound of equipment being moved and voices coming down the stairs. Time to return to the inn, Juliet decided, and moved quickly, careful not to disturb the sleeping valet. She had to reach her donkey and be gone before they reached the castle walls.

By the time James opened her door and came to check on her, Juliet was back in bed, this time her nightgown covering nothing but her bare body and her spectacles safely tucked away, out of sight. The bed creaked as James slid under the covers to join her and she pretended to roll away from him in her sleep. She heard his sigh of frustration.

Well, it was just too bad, she decided. If he wished for a wife, then he ought to treat her as if she was one, not go gallivanting off in the middle of the night without her. No, nor keep such secrets.

Still, she would have wagered neither of them slept much at all that night. Certainly Juliet knew that she did not, and judging by how often James tossed and turned as the hours wore on, neither did he. It would serve them both right, she thought with an inward growl, if they met over breakfast with foul tempers and red eyes from lack of sleep!

Chapter 19

James poured himself another cup of something the innkeeper called coffee in hopes of clearing the cobwebs of fatigue from his brain. He peered sleepily at Juliet and thought she looked a trifle peaked as well.

But that made no sense. Juliet had no reason to look as though she hadn't slept. Not when she was tucked up safe and warm in her bed every night while he was tramping up to the castle and back for Harry. He'd lost count but surely it was far too many nights in a row.

How were they even to know if the experiment succeeded? James grumbled to himself. To be sure, Harry had said there would be a man in place to report back and he was merely to try different intensities of light and lengths of exposure, but still it seemed pointless if one could not know the outcome of the experiment.

And James was not entirely certain Harry would tell him. Harry would ask for his notes and nod and thank him, but with Harry there was no knowing if he would ever tell James anything at all to the point! He was likely to find out only if there was total failure. He would know because Harry would ask him to try all over again. And what excuse he would give the next time, James could not imagine. He could not, after all, claim to need to go on a honeymoon twice with the same bride.

If Juliet would even put up with such nonsense. She was looking at him right now as if she were distinctly displeased about something. James was not at all certain he wanted to know what it might be. Her first words confirmed his instincts.

"You look tired, James," she said in what he had come to recognize as her opening gambit. "Were you out very late again?"

"Uh, somewhat," he answered cautiously.

"Were the stars very bright?"

"Uh, yes."

"What constellations did you see?"

Well, that was a new one. And James could answer that question in his sleep. Of course he could. He knew what constellations should have been visible. He just couldn't think of any at the moment.

The silence stretched on and Juliet's smile stretched thinner. Her voice took on acid tones as she said, "I wish you had shown me your telescope. Last night or the night before or any of the nights before that. Perhaps I could have suggested some way to make it work better."

"It, uh, worked fine."

"You just can't remember what you saw?"

"I, uh, that's right. I'm unaccountably tired this morning. Can't explain it, but there it is."

"Of course it is," she said in soothing tones he did not trust.

Enough was enough. James was tired of being questioned this way every morning. He decided to go on the offensive. "You look a trifle tired yourself," he said.

Now she blushed. Then tilted up her chin. "You snore," she said.

He blinked. Peered closer at her. Was she roasting him? Insulting him? She seemed to be looking everywhere except at his face.

"Should I request another room?" he asked stiffly.

"No!"

The cry, involuntary he was certain, reassured James. He smiled and decided to venture a small jest. "I shall try not to snore tonight," he said teasingly.

That brought a smile to her face and James found himself giving a tiny sigh of relief. He reached over and took her hand in his, lacing their fingers together.

"We could go back to bed," he said. "There's no one expecting us, nothing else we must do."

She blushed more deeply than before and he was afraid he had embarrassed her. He was cursing himself for being foolish beyond permission when she looked at him and he saw the joy in her eyes.

Still, her voice was perfectly calm, perfectly cool, perfectly correct as she replied, "I think that might be permissible."

But he was not deceived. This blushing bride of his, for all her oddity, was a passionate woman. He really did want, James told himself, to savor that passion.

Juliet wondered what her husband was thinking. He was looking at her in such an odd way. Had she sunk herself beneath reproach by her answer? And yet he had asked. And she did want to go back to bed with him.

Mama would tell her she was behaving scandalously and would soon give James a disgust of her, at this rate. But James didn't seem disgusted. Indeed, he was looking at her with distinct approval in his eyes.

He took her hand and led her back to their bed-chamber, where her maid and his valet were straightening the room. Both looked at the couple expectantly.

"Er, you may go," James said awkwardly.

"Do you wish for your pelisse? Or your spencer?" the maid asked brightly.

"Do you wish your overcoat, sir?" the valet chimed

in. "It looks to be brewing up a nasty wind outside, sir. I could have it out for you in a trice."

James colored up and Juliet was charmed by the sight. She watched as he stammered. "N-No. That is, er, Mrs. Langford and I thought to rest a bit."

Sudden comprehension dawned on both their faces as well as grins that were hastily suppressed. Bowing, curtseying, the two backed out of the room.

"Of course, sir."

"Yes, ma'am."

When the door closed behind them, the pair apparently thought themselves safe because both Juliet and James could hear a sudden fit of giggles from the maid and a guffaw from the valet.

James started toward the door, as though he meant to fling it open and ring a peal over the servants' heads. Juliet stopped him by placing her hand on his arm.

"They mean well," she said softly. "Indeed, I think they are happy for us."

He hesitated and she pressed her case. "I think they wish us happy and are pleased that we are beginning to act like a couple on our honeymoon. And since it seems so important to you to give everyone that impression, what could be more useful than two servants who make it clear what their master and mistress are about?"

That gave him pause—she could see it in his face. And with a sigh he drew her to him and buried his face in her hair. It was an intimate gesture, one that sent a rush of warmth all through Juliet. She risked putting her arms around him and tilting up her face to make it easy for him if he should decide he wished to kiss her.

He did. It was a gentle, tender kiss that somehow swiftly became so much more. It was as though he did not wish to succumb but could not help himself. Well, that was fine with Juliet. She did not wish him to be able to help himself either.

And when he drew her toward the bed, his fingers fumbling with the fastenings on her dress, she made no objection. Indeed, her own fingers began to deftly undo the fastenings of his shirt. He scarcely noticed, she thought, until he suddenly caught her fingers with his hand.

Alarmed she looked up at him, fearing to see shock or disapproval in his eyes. Instead she saw something that might have been, that she desperately hoped was, warmth and approval and even, perhaps affection in those fine gray eyes.

"You must stop doing that long enough to allow me to lift your gown over your head," he said, a hint of amusement in his voice.

Juliet nodded, not trusting herself to speak, and helped him remove her dress. And the garments beneath. At the same time she coaxed the shirt from his back and reached out to touch his broad chest.

Then they stood, naked as the day they were born, together in the middle of the room. As he reached for her, Juliet was astonished to realize that she felt neither distress nor embarrassment.

To be sure, she had dropped her nightshift the other morning but that had been different somehow. A challenge of sorts. This was a celebration of something special between them. And Juliet was quite sure that neither her mother, nor anyone else she knew in the *ton,* would approve. But she didn't care. Not when James so clearly did.

She reached out for him now, even as he was reaching for her. She reveled in the feel of her body against his. It was only a few steps to the bed but it seemed to take forever to get there.

Later, when they lay side by side, Juliet ventured to reach out to touch James. Instantly he captured her hand with his own and raised it to his lips, where he caressed each fingertip.

Juliet shivered but she made herself ask him anyway, "Where did you go last night? Where have you gone every night?"

He started. She could feel the tension throughout his body, pressed as close as it was to her own. Still, his voice was casual.

"To look through my telescope. I've told you so before."

"At the bell tower."

Now he frowned. Thinking. As though trying to remember what she might have overheard. At last he seemed to decide it didn't matter. He shrugged.

"Yes. The tower. Excellent viewing from there."

"Could I go with you next time?" she asked in a voice kept deliberately mild and even meek.

He hemmed and hawed and in the end stammered an apology and something about preferring to do it all on his own. Onlookers making him nervous, or some such nonsense.

Juliet pretended to believe it all.

"Oh. Of course," she said. "I understand perfectly."

She felt him relax and a surge of anger went through her own body. How dare he deceive her this way? One of these days he would find out just who the fool might be!

Still, when he reached for her, her anger was not enough to make her keep him away.

A good many hours later, the leader of the smugglers looked at his men in exasperation. Overhead the moon shone with remarkable brightness.

"Again?" he demanded. "How could they make such a mistake again? Surely they realize by now that they are looking too close to the castle and it ain't our lights they're seeing?"

The other man was careful to keep his eyes fixed

on the ground. Frustration echoed in his voice as he said, "We tried to signal 'em. But we was too late. They was already too close to them rocks. Lost one boat they did afore they realized wot was wot and sheared off and come found us where we was supposed to be."

"We did get some'at this time," another man added helpfully.

"But not the best of it," their leader muttered. "Enough is enough, I say! Before the next shipment is due, we must take care of the blasted tower lights."

"How's we gonna do that?" another of the men asked, puzzled.

The leader got a faraway look in his eyes. His expression grew very grim. "I don't know," he admitted slowly, "but somehow we will."

He paused and then suddenly pointed to a handful of men. "Tomorrow night you will all come with me and we'll scout about the castle walls. If we see the means to act, we will. Otherwise we'll look and watch and plan. I tell you this cannot and will not go on any longer. I'll not be made a fool of by anyone!"

Chapter 20

Harry sat and stared at the message in his hand. This was the answer he'd been waiting for. He knew better than to ask how the information had gotten to him so quickly, what risks had been taken to ensure that it did.

So. He had his answer. And now he must send his to James. Better yet, he would carry it himself, he decided. The fewer people involved, the better. His imminent departure for Spain would be explanation enough for stopping to visit his brother and the bride in Dover.

Harry looked at the clock. It was late to be starting out today. And yet he dared not delay. Better to ride as far as he could before dark and the rest of the way in the morning. It would not take him long to pack his things, but there were other matters to be taken care of, letters to be written before he could be on his way. And then he would need to take his leave of George and Athenia.

When Harry finally went in search of his brother sometime later, he found him in his study.

Lord Darton waved the major to a seat. "Well, what plans have you for this evening?" he asked in a jovial voice.

"I came to tell you, George, that I must be on my way back to Spain," Harry replied soberly. "My orders arrived this afternoon. My bags already are packed and in the foyer."

"So soon?" George looked shocked and his voice was querulous as he said, "I thought you fixed in London for a little while longer. Can you not at least wait until morning to leave?"

Harry shrugged and pretended to a carelessness he did not feel. "I dare not disobey orders. I think it best I leave at once. I shall stop on my way to the coast and visit James and his bride and wish them happy."

George grumbled and pushed away the pile of accounts he had been working on. "That is another match I cannot entirely like. No, nor the circumstances that led to it! But I suppose it cannot be helped. I just hope that you, Harry, will show more sense than your brothers when it comes time to wed. No unlikely and unsuitable bride for you, I pray."

"No, none," Harry agreed. "Because I do not intend to marry at all. It would be most unfair to any woman to ask her to tie her life to a man who might well be killed at any moment."

"Here! That's not what I meant!" George protested.

"No, but it is the truth, nonetheless," Harry replied. He paused and smiled, not unkindly. "Give it over, George. I will not fall prey to matchmaking. Yours or anyone else's. I mean to stay a bachelor."

"I do not like it, Harry. I do not like it at all. But I suppose," George said with heavy irony, "there is nothing I can say or do about it that will change your mind."

Now Harry grinned outright and waved his hand at Darton. "No, nothing," he agreed. "But you can wish me well. It's time I was on my way."

Both men rose to their feet and clasped hands. In a voice suspiciously husky, George, Lord Darton said, "Take care of yourself, Harry, and at least try to come back to us safe and sound."

The major smiled wryly. "I shall. If I can."

"Why the devil you had to choose such a dangerous occupation I will never understand," George continued to grumble as they walked out of the study.

"It's where we part company, you and I," Harry answered with affection patent in his voice. "Just know that it was something I had to do."

George sighed. "I do know it."

Then, before either could utter any more words that might make the leave-taking even harder, they headed for the front door.

In the foyer Athenia, Lady Darton, was waiting. Somehow she already knew that he was leaving. The servants in this house, Harry thought wryly, were a remarkably efficient source of information. Though perhaps it was his bags, standing by the door, that had given the game away.

"I wanted to wish you well, Harry," she said. Then echoing her husband's words, she added, "George and I both hope to see you back here soon, safe and well."

The major grinned unrepentantly. "I have already promised I shall try," he said.

Then as Lord and Lady Darton watched, Harry lashed his belongings to his saddle and mounted his horse. A quick salute to both of them, a word of thanks, and a coin tossed to the groom who had been holding the reins, and Harry was off.

The coast, he thought, was a long ride away, but with luck, he would reach it by noon tomorrow.

The night began like every other night when Juliet had slipped out of the inn after James. After almost two weeks of this nonsense, she was getting quite tired of these ridiculous expeditions. Especially since she had already dropped her spectacles several times and almost lost them once in the dark! It would be different if she could actually take part in the experiments he was conducting, but as it was, it was only sheer stubbornness that made her continue to follow him, night after night.

Indeed, Juliet had just about decided to go back to the inn when, as she slipped out of the tower door, she suddenly found herself surrounded by a very unsavory group of men. What on earth were they doing here? Surely it should have been safe within the castle walls? But Juliet didn't stop to think about the matter for long. She didn't even stop to recall the dagger she carried in her boot. Instead, instinct took over and she let out a most unladylike shriek.

The two men above her in the tower heard the shriek. With a shock, James recognized the voice and he was moving toward the doorway before Baines even had time to react.

In moments he was down the stairs and out the door and at Juliet's side. He arrived in time to hear her saying, "Do you think I'd be wearing breeches if the ghosts hadn't burned my dress off of me?"

The moment she said the words, Juliet knew they were a mistake. The men were bound to ask where the breeches and shirt had come from. So she kept right on talking. Perhaps if she talked fast enough, they wouldn't have time to ask that question or even, perhaps, think of it. But then, her mother always did complain that she had an impetuous tongue. For once it might prove useful.

Desperately she tried to distract the men around her. "There are ghosts here, you know. They delight in fire. And noise. It was terrible up in the tower, terrible."

And then, suddenly James was there beside her. Theatrically Juliet shivered and with a fearful moan she fainted into James's waiting arms. At least she appeared to faint. Juliet hoped she was convincing. This was not, after all, the sort of thing she had any

practice at and she did have to be careful not to dislodge her spectacles and land on them as she fell.

In any event, she appeared to have created a most
satisfactory commotion. And it was with another
shiver, this time of delight, that she heard James demand, in a masterful voice, "What the devil is going
on here?"

Now the leader of the men appeared to have recovered somewhat. At least enough to say, "That's wot
we'd loike to know! These lights. They caused some
friends of ours to land in the wrong spot. Thought
your lights was ours. Now we can't get wot they left
be'ind, it being too close to the castle wot they left it."

James blinked. Even with her eyes closed, Juliet
knew he blinked. Then he must have smiled. A seraphic smile. Finally he spoke.

"My wife is quite right. It was the ghosts. I'm an
avid investigator of ghosts, you know. And I'd heard
there were some particularly nasty ones here. But no
one told me about the lights. I collect it's a new phe-
nomenon. Started in the last week or so. I'm trying to
understand how it's done."

"Lights. Fire. Ghosts."

More than one of the men snorted in disgust. There
were a few guffaws and the leader sounded even an-
grier as he said, "Oi think you're making fun of us.
Ghosts!"

At just that moment, a light flashed overhead. Juliet
decided, as she heard the gasps around her, that this
might be a good time to recover from her faint. Besides, James must have been finding her a trifle heavy
burden by now.

She was in time to see another glow of light above,
and then still another. Then an eerie howling above
them. The men began to shift uneasily. One or two
started to slip away. The leader, however, was not so
easily daunted.

"Oi don'ts believe it's no ghost. Oi'm going up there to see."

As he opened the door to what some said had once been a Roman lighthouse, there was another flash of light and this time the sound of an explosion.

Without a word, the leader let go of the door and signaled to his men and in moments they had all slipped away. As they went, someone called out that they would be back to check the tower another time.

Juliet and James didn't care. It was enough to know the men were gone. They waited for what seemed forever, neither speaking until they were certain no one was going to return. Then James turned a stern gaze on Juliet and said, reprovingly, "Ghosts burnt your dress?"

Juliet avoided his eyes. She looked at the ground as she said, "I had to find some reason to explain why I was in breeches."

"Ah, yes, the breeches. You shall explain that one to me. Right after you explain what you are doing here at all," James said, a stern expression on his face.

But before she could answer, the door to the tower opened and the chaplain's assistant emerged. He slipped silently over to where they were and in the oddly cultured voice that was as much an anomaly as the man himself, he said, "I thought myself an excellent teller of ghost stories, madam, but you beat me all hollow."

And then he bent and kissed the back of her hand. Juliet shivered. The man was very, very strange. Mind you, he was very nice, but there was something very much out of place about the fellow too.

James turned to the chaplain's assistant and said, with a frown, "I didn't have any powder up there. How did you cause the explosion?"

The other man lifted his eyebrows and smiled. "I did. A precaution, you might say. And a notion for an experiment of my own. But the less you know, the better.''

Juliet expected James to be annoyed at the impertinence but he wasn't. He only nodded. How odd! One more strange thing to chalk up about this man who couldn't possibly be the simple chaplain's assistant that he seemed to be.

"It might be best to stop for the night, Langford,'' the man said quietly. "We cannot be certain those men will not return. Or that the noise will not bring others to investigate.''

James nodded. "First we need to find my valet. He must be around here somewhere.''

They found Woods, knocked unconscious, at the usual spot where he napped each night while James and the chaplain's assistant were busy in the tower. They managed to rouse him and he was at once mortified at his failure to warn them about the smugglers.

"Never mind,'' James said soothingly. "Let's just get you and my wife and myself back to town.''

Woods nodded and somehow managed to get to his feet. James helped support him as the four of them made their way to the small castle door they used each night for entrance. It was standing open and the chaplain's assistant and James looked at one another, a grim expression on their faces.

"This must be the way they came in. They must have seen me do so,'' James said.

The other man nodded. "Let me check that no one is still hanging about.'' A moment later he returned. "I saw no one. But your carriage is gone. They must have taken it. You'll have to go back on foot.''

Now James looked at Juliet with concern but she merely planted a hand on one hip and said, daring him to contradict her, "And my donkey is gone as well. We'd best get started walking, hadn't we?''

There was nothing he could say to that, so they did. Occasionally Woods stumbled and James had to help him, but they made it back to town. Near the edge of it, they found the carriage and horses. It looked as though the horses and carriage had not been stolen but had merely bolted, perhaps when the smugglers tried to take charge of them.

"At least it's here and undamaged," James said. "Let us get back to the inn."

"But my donkey!"

"You must hope it found its own way home for I see no donkey hereabouts, nor do I think it wise or safe for us to dally looking for it."

"I suppose you are right," Juliet reluctantly agreed.

The three climbed into the carriage for the rest of their journey back to the inn. The horses' hooves had been muffled and the wheels well greased so that they moved with very little noise. And Juliet was not altogether displeased to find herself squeezed very close to James on the seat.

Even the need to slip back into the inn unnoticed did not daunt her. Nor the way James tried to frown at her. There was too much concern patent in his fine gray eyes. Too much warmth in the way they caressed her. Perhaps, she thought, he did care after all.

Chapter 21

Over the breakfast table, James eyed Juliet warily. They'd both been too tired the night before to do anything more than fall into bed and go to sleep. But there was a look in her eyes this morning that he greatly distrusted. What the devil was he going to tell her when she started asking her questions?

But Juliet didn't ask any questions. Instead she said, "Since I do not think you were attempting to signal to smugglers, I must believe that you were trying to signal all the way across the channel."

James gaped at her, too stunned even to disagree.

Juliet dabbed daintily at her lips then went on in a disturbingly calm voice. "You have not discussed the matter with me since we were in London; nevertheless I have been thinking about it and I have one or two suggestions of how you might increase the output of light."

This, however, was too much for James. "What makes you believe that the output is the only essential factor? Perhaps I want the minimum light that will do the trick!"

He growled the words, frustration patent in his voice. Juliet's eyes opened wide. Then she reached across the table and put her hand over his. "Wonderful!" she exclaimed softly. "An even better challenge for us!"

James blinked. He started to speak and stopped. Finally his shoulders began to shake. He was laughing. He could not help himself. What else was there to do when one had a wife like Juliet?

She was not amused. "Do you think I cannot help you?" she demanded.

Abruptly he stopped laughing and placed his other hand over hers. "I think perhaps I would be foolish not to let you try," he said.

Then she smiled. "Good. Now tell me, what have you tried thus far?"

At Dover Castle, the governor of the place regarded his visitor with even greater impatience than he had greeted the gentleman from London. This fellow was, after all, only the chaplain's assistant and why should it be thought necessary that he meet with him? Except that there seemed to be some sort of mystery about the fellow. No one quite knew who had accepted the orders assigning him to Dover Castle. And there had, after all, been those odd goings-on last night around the tower.

Meanwhile, even as the governor studied him, the chaplain's assistant regarded the governor with just as much interest. There was even a certain gleam in his eyes that the governor found most disconcerting. The moment they were alone, however, the chaplain's assistant spoke first.

"Do you not remember me, Whiskers?"

The governor gaped. "Baines?" he demanded, an incredulous look on his face. He peered closer. "Damned if it isn't! Always were good at disguises, as I recall. But what are you doing here? And when on earth did you become a chaplain's assistant, anyway?"

Frederick Baines, gentleman and sometimes much more, quietly explained. At least he explained as much as he thought proper. By the time he was done, the governor had given his assurances that no one would investigate anything that occurred at the bell tower, no matter what bizarre things appeared to be happening there.

"What excuse shall I give my men?" the governor of Dover Castle asked thoughtfully.

Baines hesitated. "You've heard, no doubt, about the contretemps with smugglers last night?"

The governor was even more hesitant. And defensive. "Langford told me to order my men not to pay any attention to him. *No matter what!* And they didn't."

"Yes, yes, to be sure," Baines agreed. "Now let us use that to advantage. Let slip word that the government has decided to see if the smugglers can be confounded by having lights flashed from the bell tower."

The governor slowly nodded. "Yes, it might work. It certainly sounds plausible. Who will be doing this flashing of light? You and Langford?"

Frederick Baines smiled. "For a while. Then I'll do it alone. Eventually there will be another man to take my place. He'll be reliable and I promise I shall bring him to meet you first."

"All right." The governor paused. Then, as if he could not help himself, he asked in a burst of words, "What part does Langford have in all of this? I should think that you, of all people, would distrust old Darton's son!"

Baines hesitated again. He chose his words carefully. "There is not," he said, "everything known, I think, about that case. Suspicions, yes, but never proved. And I have reason to believe they might have been false."

It was patent the governor struggled with himself. Finally he shrugged. "If you are satisfied, I suppose there is nothing for me to cavil at. But I tell you bluntly I don't like it!"

"Yes, well, young Langford will be gone soon,"

Baines said, rising to his feet. He held out his hand to his old friend. "Thank you. It is important, you know."

The governor smiled a wry smile. "I rather thought it was, if you were involved."

Again Baines waved a careless hand. "I'm only a minor character."

The governor snorted. "Oh, sure. Just as you were a minor character in the old days, in the Mediterranean. No, no, that won't wash with me! But never mind. You've gotten what you wanted and meanwhile I've a mystery on my hands, but one, you may be sure, I shan't be foolish enough to attempt to investigate."

Baines nodded and took his leave. The governor was left to explain to his aide de camp that the chaplain's assistant who had just left was rather more important than he seemed and that he was to be given all possible assistance should he ask for it. Just why the chaplain's assistant was important the governor left to his aide's imagination, although he did indeed hint that it had to do with stopping smugglers.

James rose to his feet at the sight of Harry coming into their private parlor. He blinked several times then said, "What is it, Harry? Surely you are not calling off the experiment so soon?"

The major shook his head. "No. Quite the opposite. We have sufficient results. My contact got word to me yesterday. The experiment was a complete success."

The next several minutes were spent with Harry and James talking over which signals had been most effective and whether they ought to be refined even further.

As they were talking, Juliet came into the room. Instantly Harry fell silent. Both men rose to their feet. A tiny frown creased her brow as she greeted them.

Harry shot a significant look at James then bowed

and said, "I must take my leave now. I trust you understand everything?"

"The signals, you mean," Juliet said in a knowing way.

At Harry's look of dismay, James hastened to say, "She caught us at it. But she's been a great help, truly she has, and she won't gossip. Will you, my love?"

For a long moment she gazed at him with a dazed look in her eyes. "Did you call me love?" she asked, in a voice that was not altogether steady.

He nodded—bravely, Harry thought. She took a deep breath and then turned to the major. "You needn't worry. I understand fully the need for secrecy. I'm not such a fool that I can't keep a still tongue in my head."

Harry made up his mind in an instant. He bowed to her again and said, a wry smile quirking at the corners of his mouth, "I never thought you were."

He offered her a cup of coffee. Unfortunately, somehow, in doing so, he managed to spill some on her dress. To his chagrin, she did not leave the room to change but settled for mopping at it with a napkin.

Harry sighed inwardly and gave it up as a bad cause. Clearly he was not going to be rid of her and perhaps it was just as well. If she were to prove as resourceful as Philip's wife, she might be useful at some point.

His thoughts were so occupied that at first he did not hear James. And then, when he did, the words seemed to make no sense.

"Please wait a moment, Harry. I've got to go and get Father's mirror."

The major looked at Juliet. She looked away and bit her lower lip. Apparently, as odd as James had sounded, she at least understood what he meant.

Fortunately for Harry's peace of mind, James returned shortly. But instead of carrying a mirror, he held out a letter to Harry.

The major took it and started to read. He was rather

astonished to find it was in French, but his facility with
languages was something of a legend in the family and
he made the translation even quicker than Juliet had
done. He looked up sharply at both of them, his
face pale.

"How and where was this found?" he asked, with
an indrawn breath.

James and Juliet looked at one another. Finally she
said, "I dropped the mirror."

"Mirror?"

"Father's mirror. From his dressing case," James
explained. "I've never liked the thing. Far too ornate
for my taste. So I've never used it. Apparently it had
a false back and the letter was hidden inside."

"Have you read it?" Harry asked.

"I have," Juliet said. "And I found it most
disturbing."

"Why the devil would Father have had such a letter
in his possession?" James demanded. "He had no love
for the French! Yes, yes, I know he championed the
rights of the poor, but he never felt England ought to
go the way of France! Not after they murdered all
those people."

"So far as we know, he did not champion the
French," Harry replied, a grim edge to his voice. "But
can we be certain? This is a most damning letter."

He looked again at the letter, paying particular attention to the signature. He shook his head, more than
once. Finally he handed the letter back to James.

"Keep this safe," Harry said. "I would take it with
me but I think it better not to do so. I will, however,
ask about and see if I can discover anything. I cannot
believe it means what it seems to mean but I will allow
that it makes me uneasy."

"Nor I," James agreed. He paused, then asked with
patent concern in his voice, "You will be discreet? If
anyone else were to learn of this letter, it would be
the most appalling scandal."

Harry smiled and it was not a pretty smile. "No one shall know a thing," he said in a voice that made both Juliet and James shudder.

And then he was himself again, the carefree young officer. Major Harry Langford bowed lightly, gallantly, then said, "I must be going. I thank you, James, and you, Juliet, for all your assistance."

"Where do you go from here?" Juliet had the temerity to ask.

Harry smiled a seraphic smile. He waved a hand carelessly. "To the castle. Perhaps pay my respects to the governor. And then, why then I might walk about a bit and visit the church and the bell tower."

Then, with another bow and more words of polite leave-taking, Harry was gone.

Harry knelt in the church. He prayed with the fervor of a man who knew he might be going to his death. He prayed with the fervor of one who knew he might be observed.

And he was. He had scarcely risen to his feet when someone came up the aisle toward him. "May I help you?" the man asked gently.

They recognized each other at perhaps the same moment. A matching smile lit both faces briefly. Then the same wariness, the same cautious gaze around to make certain they were not being watched.

"I am the chaplain's assistant here," Frederick Baines said with unctuous concern. "Perhaps you would like to have me point out the features of our little chapel?"

"I should like that very much," Harry replied gravely. "I have not seen it before."

Then, as they made the circuit of the small church, they talked softly, so softly no one standing even two feet away could have overheard what they were saying.

"It worked?"

"Marvelously well. The French presumed it to be smugglers."

"Here the smugglers presumed it to be ghosts."

The two men smiled for a moment at one another, then resumed their discourse. It centered, for a bit, on intensity of light and length of time it was safe to be sending messages and how often.

Then, "You will undertake to supervise this side of things?"

Frederick Baines bowed. "I have already arranged to be responsible for the bell tower. No one will question what I do up there."

"Good. You know I am very grateful to you for your part in this."

Baines smiled a wry smile. "I liked your father. He would have wanted me to help you."

At the mention of the late Lord Darton, Harry's expression grew grim. Of a sudden he was no longer so certain Baines was the right person to whom he should entrust the task of overseeing the signaling.

The other man put a hand on Harry's arm. Softly he said, "You had best go. It would not do to draw attention to the connection between us."

In an instant Harry made up his mind. Letter or no letter, he could not believe his father had been a traitor. And even if he were, Frederick Baines had served the government well in the Mediterranean and there was no reason to believe he would not do so again, here.

Harry nodded. "Thank you for all your assistance," he said. "I will send you word, if necessary, through the same channels as before."

Baines bowed gravely, as though giving a benediction to the young soldier going off to war, and then they parted, Harry striding purposefully out of the church and Baines moving to carry out his duties as assistant to the chaplain of the church.

In one of the more disreputable inns to be found in Dover, a group of men sat and grumbled amongst themselves.

"I tell you there's no such thing as ghosts!"

"You wouldn't say so if you had been there."

"Even if there are, them two was up in the tower more'n one night and the ghosts didn't bother 'em none."

"They must'a been laughing their heads off thinking about how we run away," one man said slyly.

That earned him a glare from their leader, but he could tell his words had hit their mark. It would take time, but their leader was not a man to take defeat lightly. There would be something done, there would. And none too soon, he thought with grim satisfaction.

Chapter 22

～

When they were alone in the parlor again, Juliet turned to James. There was a hint of wistfulness in her gaze as she said, "So the experiment is over? And just as I was finally about to be able to help you?"

James nodded absently, his mind on other things.

Juliet tried again. "Will you need to collect your equipment?"

"No, I shall leave it for the man at the tower to use. Harry will explain everything to the fellow; we need not go within the castle walls again."

Really, it was very provoking, Juliet thought, feeling suddenly unaccountably shy. She started to speak again but then James looked at her in such a way, with such anguish in his eyes, that she actually took a step backward.

"James, what is the matter?"

He looked at her and gave a sigh of patent exasperation. "I do not wish to feel the way I do," he said. "I do not wish to blame you for finding the letter, for making both Harry and myself doubt our father. But I find that I cannot help doing so."

Shaken, Juliet reached out a hand toward him. "James, I'm sorry! Had I known—"

"Had you known, you would not have dropped the mirror?" James demanded. "I am sorry but it is too late for that. But in the future I shall expect you to leave my possessions alone. And should you ever find a second letter, I hope to God you may have the sense to burn it."

"But you said I should not!" she protested.

"Perhaps," he said, "I was mistaken."

And then he turned on his heel and headed for the door.

"James!" she called out after him.

He paused and looked at her over his shoulder. "Yes?"

Her expression ought to have melted his reserve. It did not. And when she saw that it did not, Juliet dropped the hand she was holding out to him.

"I did not think, indeed you told me you were not, a man who would run from the truth," she said.

And because, in general he was not, James left the private parlor all that much the faster. Behind him, just before he closed the door, he heard her sink onto a chair and he knew, even without looking, that there would be an expression of despair on her face.

But he could not bring himself to care.

Whom could he talk with about this? No one! He dare not let anyone else know about the letter. Certainly not George. Perhaps Philip. But Philip was back in London. And to be sure, Harry had said they could go back to London, that Baines would take over the signaling at the bell tower, but James found himself strangely reluctant to tell yet another brother what he had found.

It went against the grain to give even a moment's credence to the notion that his father had been a traitor. And yet the letter was damning. As was the fact that his father had kept it hidden in the back of a mirror. If the correspondence had been an innocent thing, why hide it at all?

Lost in these thoughts, James wandered about the town aimlessly. At some point he finally noticed the whispering, and just as he realized the voices sounded a great deal like those of the smugglers from the night before, something struck the back of his head.

Juliet was not a patient woman. When James did not return to the inn within the hour, she decided, perhaps unwisely, to go looking for him. She questioned Woods closely but he swore that Mr. Langford had told him nothing of what he intended, nothing of where he meant to go save that he was certain he had not gone up to the castle.

It was irrational, Juliet knew, but she began to grow worried. She would have spoken with James's brother Harry but that would have meant trying to seek him out at Dover castle. Even if she could find him there, what would she say? That she and James had had a fight? Harry had a ship to catch. She could not risk causing him to miss it when she had no better cause than this.

Instead, she decided, she would walk about the town and see if she could find James. But not in a gown stained with coffee.

In her distraction, Juliet put on one of the silliest gowns her mother had made her order. One that had been packed with the new ones simply because there had been nothing else to do with it when they decamped from the hotel in London.

Except that it was not precisely distraction that made Juliet choose that dress. Rather, her thought was that if she seemed a mere, silly female, then she would be able to ask any question she wished, of anyone, and they would answer her without thinking greatly about the matter or take great note of her having done so.

So, dressed in far more frills than she normally could tolerate, Juliet sallied forth to look for James. In one hand she carried her reticule, in the other a frilly parasol, ostensibly to shield her from the sun but in truth because she knew that it had a daunting effect on overly impertinent males when used to good purpose.

Walking out on her own, she feared she might run into just such discourteous fellows. And if that were not sufficient, she had, at the last moment, tucked her dagger into the bodice of her dress. To be sure, it was a trifle uncomfortable there, but she wanted it easily to hand if there was trouble and this way it was entirely out of sight.

The one incongruous note in her appearance was her spectacles perched firmly upon her nose. Juliet knew they did not match the frills and parasol, but if she was to find James, she must be able to see. And to the devil with anyone who dared to laugh at her, she vowed!

No one did laugh. Indeed, no one seemed to pay her any attention at all. And unfortunately, once she was more than a few steps from the inn, Juliet could find very few people who remembered seeing James. It was really most distressing.

And then she noticed the boy. He was a raggedly dressed street urchin but he was looking about him with the shrewdest eyes she had ever seen.

On impulse she said, "Have you seen a man who stood this tall, with brown hair and gray eyes? A gentleman dressed in elegant clothing but his neckcloth a trifle askew?"

"The one wot got bopped on the 'ead?" the boy asked. "The one wot the smugglers was saying they was mad at? Sumfing about lights and ghosts and such?"

Juliet closed her eyes, breathed a tiny prayer, and opened them again. "Yes," she said, nodding her head vigorously, "that gentleman."

The boy pointed. "They took 'im there."

Juliet looked. She saw a dirty inn that did not in the least seem inviting. She shuddered. But if James was there, she had to rescue him. If he had indeed gotten "bopped on the head," he would be in no condition to rescue himself.

But how, precisely, was she to do so? That was the question that worried Juliet. The inn was not the sort of place that a lady would willingly enter, and if she did so, it would certainly put the smugglers on their guard.

As she watched the inn, brooding, Juliet noticed that a few women did enter the establishment. Women Juliet's mother would have indignantly said she should not deign to notice.

But Juliet did notice them. With great interest. Suddenly she knew what she must do. She looked around and whisked herself into the nearest alley. There she tugged at the bosom of her dress, trying to lower it. To no avail. With growing frustration she tugged harder and succeeded in ripping some of the ruffled material at the neckline. Which gave her an even more outrageous notion.

She took the dagger that lay concealed in a small sheath between her breasts and used it to cut off all the lace and furbelows at the neckline of her dress. When even that did not seem enough, she cut the dress itself until it opened low enough to match what the other women wore.

Would that do? she asked herself.

Juliet chewed her lower lip, looking down. Her hem. The hem of her dress ought to be shorter. She didn't hesitate but began to cut off the lowest flounce on her hem. That shortened things quite a bit, showing her trim ankles quite nicely. Unfortunately, in removing the flounce, the seam at the side of her skirt also tore, revealing even more of her legs—to a degree that was really quite shocking.

A sparkle lit Juliet's eyes and she grinned to herself, then promptly slit the other side as well. That, she thought with satisfaction, ought to distract the smugglers nicely! Now what to do with the dagger? She had cut her dress so low in front that she could no longer conceal it there. Well, she thought with a frown, she would just have to tie it onto her leg, higher than the slit in the sides of her skirt, of course. She could use some of the discarded fabric from her dress to do so.

Abruptly she realized the boy was still with her, watching with something akin to awe in his eyes.

"Gorm," he said, "are you mad?"

Juliet smiled at him. "No. At least I don't think so. I just have a husband to rescue."

His eyes grew even wider and Juliet tossed him a coin and thanked him for his help. She took a deep breath and tucked her spectacles safely into her reticule. Then, resolutely, before she could change her mind and let fear overrule her, Juliet strode out of the alley. She sauntered toward the inn, imitating as best she could the walk of the women she had seen.

Inside the inn, however, Juliet had to pause and allow her eyes to adjust to the small amount of light that filtered through dingy windows that were so dirty they had to be that way on purpose. And as she looked around the room, the room looked at her.

There. In the corner. Surely those were the same men who had confronted her and James near Dover Castle? She started toward them, again trying to imitate the walk of the women she had seen. It felt very strange to allow her hips to move in such a provocative way!

One of them rose to meet her as she approached their table and she saw, with some satisfaction, that it was the leader.

"Hallo, ducky," he said, admiringly. "You're new, aren't you?"

Juliet made herself smile and lean toward him. "Very new," she said, with what was meant as a purring sound.

"Won't you join us?" he asked, waving a hand to indicate his group.

One of the other men made a strangled sound, drawing the leader's attention and a frown. "But she's the one!" the man hissed. "The one wot we saw at the castle!"

Juliet silently cursed the man's perceptiveness but she kept her smile firmly in place even as the leader swiftly surveyed her again. Once warned, she had little hope he would not recognize her as well. And he did.

Instead of the polite invitation issued moments before, he seized her arm and thrust Juliet into the nearest chair. "How very interesting," he said. "Now we have both of you."

Juliet drew in a breath. She let it out softly. "So you do have him. I thought you might. Not that he will do you any good."

That got the leader's attention. "What do you mean?" he asked sharply.

Juliet allowed herself to sigh. "He is a fool, my poor husband. A terrible fool. But he does have powerful friends and family. If he goes missing for more than a day, they will put all their power into finding him and punishing whoever they discover to be responsible."

The leader stroked his chin, patently skeptical. "I see," he said. "What I should like to know is what you are doing here. And how you come to be dressed the way you are. Ladies do not belong in this place."

As he said these last words, the leader waved a hand to indicate the inn. Juliet narrowed her eyes and said, "Ladies do not belong near Dover Castle, either. But I was there. Do you honestly think I would have let my fool of a husband go out at night alone? He'd more than likely have tumbled over a cliff if I hadn't been there. Just as he managed to be captured by you when he went out alone today."

The leader narrowed his own eyes. "You are my captive, too," he pointed out.

"Yes, but I choose to be here. I must presume my husband did not," Juliet countered.

"Choose? Why would you choose to be here?" one of the other men objected.

"Yes, why would you choose to be here?" the leader asked, regarding her with patent suspicion.

"Well, you may either believe that I have lost my wits or that I have a proposal that will make all of us wealthy."

"Proposal!"

The men scoffed. The leader stroked his chin. "You are already wealthy," he objected.

Juliet shrugged. "One cannot be too wealthy," she pointed out.

"Why do you need us?" someone demanded.

Juliet smiled. "I am a woman. And not an overly strong one. I know where there is treasure to be found, but I shall need help in, shall we say, liberating it from its current owners?"

They gaped at her. Understandably, she supposed, but still it was unnerving.

"How would you know where to find treasure?" the leader scoffed.

Juliet shrugged. "I told you I dare not let that fool of a husband of mine go out alone. He tramps across moors and pokes into caves and all sorts of odd places. Nor does he care for anything other than rocks and strange creatures and looking through lenses and such. I, on the other hand, tend to notice chests and boxes and things."

Her words had the ring of truth, for while it had not happened, she could well imagine James behaving in just such a way and herself stumbling over treasure chests and boxes of valuables.

In any event, her words were sufficiently enticing for the leader to wish to believe her. "And why come to me?" he asked.

Juliet shrugged and allowed a note of petulance to

creep into her voice. "My husband has this foolish notion that one ought not to take things which belong to others. And the most distressing tendency to tell his family about what I say. So it seems to me that if I wish to profit from what I know, I need someone strong enough to help me who will not cavil at what I wish to do."

For a long moment the men stared at her and matters hung in the balance. Juliet held her breath. But then they laughed, starting with the leader.

Juliet pretended to take offense at his amusement and he took a few moments to soothe her. Then, serious again, he asked the question she hoped he would ask.

"What, precisely, do you wish from me? And what do I get in return for my help?"

"Not a great deal," she said, keeping her eyes on the table top, for fear she would betray herself. "Simply the help of your men to retrieve the boxes and chests and such. And I presume you would know how to dispose of them to the greatest profit to all of us. Since I know the locations, I should receive at least half of the profit and all of you may split the rest."

That provoked cries of outrage, as she knew it would, and quite successfully diverted their attention from any suspicions they might have. Eventually Juliet allowed herself to be bargained down to thirty percent for her share. Then, in a small voice and with a tiny frown between her eyes she said, "But you had best release my husband. If he goes missing much longer, we shall have all kinds of soldiers down upon our heads. You ought to release him and then, in a little while, I shall follow him and he need never know of our particular arrangement."

They didn't like the suggestion, of course.

"Why not just kill him and be done with it?"

"Because," she said, her voice harsh, "if anything happens to my husband, there are those who would never rest until they had exacted revenge on whoever was responsible."

"How do we know he won't lead them straight back here?" someone else demanded.

Juliet hesitated. How to answer that one. Then she let herself smile a sardonic smile. "My husband? Admit that he was bested? I scarcely think he would do such a thing. Not when he knows it would make him the laughingstock of all who know him. No, I can promise you he will return to our lodgings and keep everything to himself. No doubt the moment he sees me he will invent some excuse why we must leave Dover at once. He will tell no one what has occurred, I assure you. It would hurt his pride too much to do so!"

There were still more protests, but the leader could see the merit in what she had said. Juliet suspected that he also thought he might be able to cheat her entirely of her share of the profit if she could not slip away from James long enough to claim it.

But at last he nodded and gave the necessary orders. Then he leaned toward her, as two of his men left the room, and said softly, "Perhaps you and I ought to go upstairs and discuss this further in private."

Juliet's eyes narrowed. Her first instinct was to refuse. Her second was that with the knife strapped to her thigh, she would be in no danger, and if the men thought their leader engaged in, er, discussions with her, then she might be able to slip out and make certain James was free.

So she let her eyes widen again and she smiled and said, with a purr in her voice, "Why not?"

Chapter 23

$\backsim\!\!\!\!\!\sim$

James came awake with a groan. His head ached and he felt bruised, as though someone had used him none too gently. He touched a hand to his head and it came away sticky. Blood. His own, he presumed from the way he felt.

What the devil had happened? He had been careless, obviously. Men. But who? He could think of only one group of men who might bear him ill will—the smugglers.

He forced himself to a sitting position and groaned again with the pain. He tried to survey his surroundings. The light was dim but it seemed to James that the room was small and there were some barrels here with him. A storeroom then. If so, then sooner or later surely someone must come to replenish their supplies. He must try to be ready to escape when they did so.

To that end, James tried to force himself to his feet. Eventually he managed to do so, even though he had to cling to the nearest barrel to keep himself from tumbling right over again.

He risked one step, and then another. A short time later he was sufficiently stable on his feet that he was able to pace the length and breadth of his prison. For it was a prison. He had found the door and it was securely locked. The prison itself was somewhat larger than he had thought and above him he could hear sounds of merrymaking. He was probably under a tavern then.

He thought of trying to attract attention by making noise, but he was rather dubious that anyone who favored this place would take his side rather than that of those who had brought him here. No, he'd best depend upon himself. Perhaps he could pick the lock?

James was in the midst of just this endeavor, and he fancied he was soon to succeed, when he heard footsteps on the other side of the door. Immediately he moved a little away from the door and slumped to the floor as though he were unconsciousness.

The door opened. A gruff voice called to him. Then a boot none too gently turned him over. He allowed himself to groan.

Rather impatiently the other voice said, "Up on yer feet! Yer to be set free. If ye'll go now. And right quick about it ye'd better be."

James didn't quite trust the man, but the chance was too good to ignore. He let his eyes flutter open. He let himself slowly rise to a seated position. He spoke in befuddled tones as he pretended to confusion.

"Where am I? What happened?"

"Never mind all that. Does ye wish to go or not?"

Now James rose to his feet, albeit he allowed himself to wobble as he did so. He touched his head with one hand. "Yes, yes, I do wish to leave," he said.

He allowed the other man to help support him, particularly as they negotiated the steep, narrow steps upward to street level. Only when he was safely out the back door and into the alleyway and all alone did he shake off his apparent confusion and take to his heels as rapidly as he could.

He had gone only a short distance, two streets away perhaps, when he realized a raggedly dressed boy was keeping at his side. He frowned at the urchin.

"Please, sir. Where is the lady?" the urchin asked, tugging at James's coat when he slowed.

James came to an abrupt halt. "What lady?"

"The lady wot went to rescue you," the urchin replied with wide open eyes.

The boy was still holding on to James's coat but James scarcely noticed. "Describe her to me," he commanded.

Juliet. It must be Juliet. The urchin's few shrewd words confirmed that. He could not fathom why she had come after him or how she had managed to find him at all. Nor by what means she had thought she could rescue him. But he was, undeniably, free.

Immediately James turned back toward the inn. Still the urchin kept pace with him. They must have Juliet. Had she traded herself for him? The thought sent a chill straight through him. How, he wondered, was he to rescue her? Perhaps a distraction? Perhaps the boy could help?

The leader of the smugglers gestured for Juliet to precede him into what appeared to be a private parlor. She did so, careful to put some distance between them.

"Wine?" he asked. "Brandy, perhaps. An excellent French one, I can vouch for it personally."

He laughed at his own jest. Juliet tried to smile. "No, I am not thirsty, thank you."

He moved closer and licked his lips. "No? Mayhap you've other appetites you'd prefer to satisfy? Well, I'm willing, m'lady, if you is. And mayhap even if you isn't."

He kept moving toward her, his intent unmistakable. Juliet moved away.

"I thought you had matters you wished to discuss in private," she countered.

"These is those matters."

"I meant the location of the caves. The treasures," she said, a hint of desperation in her voice.

That did give him pause. But then he shook his head and leered. "We can talk about that after, me love," he said, again moving toward her.

It was time, Juliet decided, to use her knife. She bent down and, through the slit in the side of her skirt, reached for the knife strapped to her thigh.

The smuggler laughed and Juliet froze. "I knew you was only playing shy!" he crowed in triumph.

Suddenly a shout went up from below. "Fire! Fire!"

"Later, me darling," the smuggler said. "You can lift your skirts for me later. For now I'd best go find out what the trouble might be."

Juliet gaped after him. She wanted to protest that she would never lift her skirts for him. But she had to allow that that was how it must have looked. And before she could gather her wits, he was gone, the door slammed shut behind him. Quickly she checked. It was locked. Well, that would prove no difficulty for her! How many times, after all, had Mama locked her in to prevent her going out to the carriage house to work on things out there?

No, the lock was no problem for Juliet. But then she suffered a check. She still could not open the door. They must, she thought, have barred it from the outside. Tendrils of smoke coming under the door fed her panic. The hinges? Perhaps she should remove the hinges?

There was no time to waste. Juliet worked quickly, trying to ignore her fear. She alternated between pounding on the door, shouting for someone to let her out, and working on the hinges. If the inn truly was on fire, they might very well forget she was there.

And then Juliet heard what she thought must be the most welcome sound in the world.

"Juliet? Are you in there?"

"James! Thank God you're free! Yes, unbar the door! Quickly, I pray you!"

It seemed to take forever. She knew it took only a moment. And then he was there. Holding out his arms to her. Except he wasn't. He was gaping at her.

"What happened to your dress?" he gasped.

"Never mind that," she said impatiently, "we've got to get out of here!"

That shook him out of his momentary shock and he grabbed her arm, pulling her toward a back stairway and down and out through the side door of the inn. "I had a boy set the fire in the storerooms near the back," he explained.

There was a great deal of smoke in the air and even greater confusion. It was no trouble to slip away through the crowd and back toward their inn. As they moved, James stripped off his jacket and insisted that Juliet put it on to cover up her dress. When she refused on the grounds that it would draw more attention than if she simply brazened things out as she was, he growled certain things she strongly suspected it was better she not hear.

They had a companion. Actually two. One was the boy who had helped both of them.

"Kin I come wif you?" the urchin asked.

Without slowing in the least, James said impatiently, "Of course not. Your mother would no doubt, er, miss you."

" 'aven't got a mother. 'aven't got a father, neither."

His words, said so bravely, with only the slightest quaver in his voice, tugged at Juliet. She looked at James. He sighed.

"Yes. Very well. You may come with us. I don't suppose you know anything about horses?"

"No, sir."

"How to be a servant of any kind?"

"No, sir."

The voice grew progressively smaller and glummer.

"Never mind," Juliet said, as reassuringly as she could, "we shall find something for you to do, won't we, James?"

"What? Er, yes, of course we will," he agreed.

But what? Juliet could feel his silent question, for it was precisely what she was asking herself.

By this time they were approaching the inn and getting some very strange looks indeed! Still the urchin persisted. "Wot will you find for me to do, sir?"

Juliet recognized only too well the look of exasperation on James's face. If she could have thought of a way to intervene, she would have done so but she could think of nothing to say. What were they going to do with the child?

"Is there anything you are good at? Anything you like to do?" James demanded.

Hesitation. Unexpected hesitation. Then the child said, with an odd diffidence, "I likes to fix things, sir."

Juliet came to an abrupt halt, almost stumbling over her feet as she did so. Beside her, she felt rather than saw James do the same.

"You like to fix things?" she echoed.

"Yes'm."

Juliet and James looked at each other, their mouths gaping open. Then they grinned singularly foolish grins at one another. Then they grinned at the boy, who started to back away, having evidently decided they were completely wanting in wits.

"Wait!" James called, holding out his hand to the boy. "We like to fix things too."

Now it was the child's turn to gape at them. "Even 'er?" he finally blurted out, pointing at Juliet.

"Even her," James confirmed, his shoulders shaking with silent laughter.

Juliet nudged her spouse aside. To the urchin she said, briskly, "We do indeed like to fix things. And that means you could prove very useful to us. If you are willing to learn and help."

"Oh, I am," he answered with a fervency they could not doubt.

"Good. Then go inside and ask for Mr. Langford's valet, Woods. Tell him we said he is to take you in charge for the moment," James told the urchin.

The boy hesitated. "Sir? There's some'un else."

That was all he said. But they could see he was holding the hand of a girl. She was older than he, but it was clear he had appointed himself her protector. She seemed almost to shrink away from them and would have disappeared if the boy had let go of her hand.

"Who is she?" James asked. "Your sister?"

The boy hesitated, then shook his head. "Me friend. I'll not go wifout 'er. 'Er father was one of them men. 'E beats 'er somefing fierce. I won't leave 'er be'ind."

James looked at Juliet. She looked at the boy. "That's why you were watching the inn, isn't it? Because you were worried about her?"

The boy nodded. Juliet looked at James. "I do not see how we can be angry with him for wanting to protect the girl," she said. "Indeed, I cannot help but think that you would have done the same, in his place. It is to his credit that he cared enough to wish to protect her, is it not?"

James hesitated. He could not deny it. "But what are we to do with a girl?" he asked. "Turn her into a housemaid? Put her to work in the kitchens? We haven't even a household yet."

"She can sew," the boy told them eagerly. "A right good talent she 'as."

"But we don't need a seamstress," James said impatiently. "What else can she do?"

The boy scuffed his foot in the dirt, not answering. Juliet put a hand on her husband's arm. "I think I know a lady who could employ the girl," she said slowly. "And this woman would understand about the need to get away from her father." To the girl she said, "How old are you?"

"Seventeen."

Juliet nodded decisively. "Old enough, then, to be leaving your father's care. Mrs. Wise will be very happy to have your help, I should think. It is all right with you, isn't it, James? Mrs. Wise is the woman I told you about, in London, who made my new dresses."

At that the girl eyed her odd attire doubtfully but James nodded. "Yes, I do remember. And you are right. It might answer very well." He stopped and looked at the boy and the girl. In a kindly voice he said, "Yes, of course the girl may come. What are your names?"

"Daniel and Abigail, sir."

"Well, Daniel and Abigail, my valet, Mr. Woods, will look after the both of you for the moment. Ask for him inside. And for heaven's sake, try to keep the girl out of sight in case her father comes looking for her!"

Then, almost as an afterthought, James tossed the boy a coin and said, "Get yourselves something to eat while you are at it."

Daniel caught the coin in midair, thanked them profusely, then tugged at Abigail's hand and disappeared into the inn with her, as though afraid the couple might change their minds. Neither James nor Juliet could blame him. Nothing they had done so far this day, after all, could have given the child any impression other than that they were a very strange pair.

Conscious of all the stares they were attracting, Juliet hurried into the inn and up the stairs to their room. James followed, his tread becoming heavier with each step. Juliet began to dread the confrontation she had a sinking feeling they were about to have.

Sure enough, the moment the door was closed behind them, James crossed his arms over his chest and said, "I trust you have an explanation for your out-landish appearance?"

"I most certainly do!" Juliet replied. "I was trying to rescue you. And it appears my ruse succeeded."

"What ruse? Pretending to be a . . . a woman of the streets?"

"Precisely. Except, well, the smuggler recognized me," Juliet added, a trifle mournfully.

His shoulders shook. Was he laughing at her? Perhaps, but if so he recovered quickly and took a step toward her, anger not laughter in his eyes.

"How dare you behave in such a way?" he demanded. "If I needed rescuing, it was for me to rescue myself!"

Juliet rolled her eyes. "Oh, to be sure. Locked in with a bar at the door, I've no doubt you were going to rescue yourself," she said in a scathing voice.

"Well, I might have," he insisted. "But we shall never know, shall we?" He paused, then curiosity got the better of him. "How did you persuade them to let me go?"

She told him. She could not resist a tiny sigh as she said, "The leader of the smugglers seemed to find me quite feminine."

James looked at her in a way that made her feel very odd inside. In a voice that was husky with emotion he said, "So do I."

And then he told her his side of the story. By the end, they were no longer on opposite sides of the room, no longer giving each other angry looks. "We ought to report them," Juliet said firmly. "There must be a magistrate or constable or someone we could tell."

James hesitated. "That might not be wise," he said slowly. "We do not wish to draw such attention to ourselves or what we have been doing up at the castle."

"But what if they attack us again?"

"I do not think that likely. I should think it more plausible that they will leave Dover with the greatest haste. Or at least disband for now."

"Do you think so?" she asked doubtfully. "I cannot like the thought that they will go unpunished."

"I think perhaps," James grinned again, "that our friend, the chaplain's assistant, may be able to have something to say to that. I shall send a note with Woods up to Dover Castle and let him know what happened. He will do whatever is right and necessary."

"I suppose that will do."

Her voice was hesitant. It was very difficult to think clearly when James held her hand in such a way and gently, absentmindedly, stroked the back of it with his thumb as he was now doing. But he seemed to have no trouble thinking or speaking.

"I did, when I first saw you, with your dress so altered," he said diffidently, "wonder if you had lost your wits. Or I had mistaken your character."

Juliet snatched her hand out of his. "Indeed?" she asked, a martial glint in her eyes. "Was it not obvious that only the most dire straits would have driven me to such a thing?"

Balked of her hand, James traced a pattern on the bed with the tip of his finger. "I did not think it for long," he offered as apology.

"Even a moment was too long!"

He looked at her, his expression solemn. "Yes, but you see, I have been thinking. It is very easy to mistake appearances. The smugglers were mistaken, they believed in your disguise."

"They did not know me," Juliet said, still glowering.

He brightened. "Precisely! And I have been thinking, you see, that perhaps the Frenchman who wrote that letter did not know my father very well."

Juliet blinked, then her mind raced along with his. "So perhaps your father was also playing a role and the Frenchman was deceived?"

James nodded. "Try as I might, I cannot believe my father would have consorted with the rebels. He valued life too highly, had too great a sense of honor, and I know that he was appalled by the deaths from the revolution."

"Perhaps the letter was not even meant for him," Juliet said slowly. "Could he have obtained it from someone else? Intercepted it, perhaps? You suggested such a thing before and intrigue does appear to run in your family."

James did not answer at once. Indeed, he seemed lost in his thoughts for several long moments. Juliet reached out and placed her hand over his.

"Trust your own heart, James," she said. "If you believe that your father could not have been a traitor, then trust that feeling and look for other answers. We have already thought of two possibilities and there may well be more."

A wry smile appeared on James's lips. He pulled Juliet to him and kissed her soundly. In a voice oddly unsteady he said, "Bless you, my love! I think you have given me my father back!"

Juliet did not perfectly understand what James was talking about, but at the moment it did not matter. What mattered was that the trouble between them seemed to be at an end, at least judging by the enthusiasm with which James was embracing her.

And when his hands began to undo the fastenings of her gown, Juliet made not the least objection. Indeed, she began to work on his shirt buttons.

"What shall we do about the letter?" Juliet asked, her head resting on James's bare shoulder.

He stroked her hair even as he said, "I would tell Harry about our thoughts but no doubt he is long gone. And he may figure it out himself. In any event, it does not matter. The letter can in no way affect him before he returns again to England. But I think perhaps I shall ask Sir Thomas about my father's activities. It is possible that he knows more than he has ever said. Sir Thomas, after all, seems to know the oddest things."

Juliet nodded, perfectly content with this reply. After all, it left her free to concentrate on the matter at hand. Which was James.

Hesitantly she asked, "You don't regret marrying me, James, do you?"

He gaped at her. Then he pulled her even closer. With a firmness in his voice that she could not doubt he said, "Never! And how you can ask, after what we have just shared, is beyond me."

Juliet traced a path on his bare chest with her fingertip. In a small voice she said, "I did not think so but I had to ask. This marriage was not, after all, what either of us had planned."

With a growl James hugged Juliet so tight that she could scarcely breathe. "I shall never regret marrying you," he said. "Indeed, I shall be grateful every day of my life to be wed to you." He paused then added softly, "Juliet, I did not, could not, know beforehand how right our marriage would be. But never doubt that I feel the most fortunate man in the world because of you."

He held her eyes with his and Juliet caught her breath at the intensity, the sincerity she read there. And then she reached out to bring his face closer to hers and she kissed James with a fierce intensity of her own.

"I," she said softly, "am the most fortunate woman!"

And then, they had no further need for words.

Chapter 24

Margaret and Woods received the news that they were to return to London without the least change of expression. It did not go unnoticed by James and Juliet, however, that their eyes strayed more than once to the rumpled bed.

"To what address will we be going, sir?" Woods did venture to ask.

James colored up. "I have not yet heard from my man of business," he admitted.

"You have been distracted by other matters," Juliet said soothingly.

"Yes, but if we do not return to London, then where are we to go?" James replied. "I cannot think it wise to linger here in Dover."

Juliet hesitated. Then drawing him over to the window on the far side of the room so that neither Margaret nor Woods would overhear, she asked, "Do you think perhaps we could visit some of the factories that have your inventions? And then you could show them to me? While your man of business finds us a house in London."

"Are you certain that is the sort of wedding trip you wish?" he asked doubtfully.

"I think that I should like it above all else," she replied. "It is part of you and something that I hope, in the future, we shall share."

He smiled down at her wryly. "Then that is what we shall do. And perhaps we could also stop and visit your parents first. I think I should like to see the place where you grew up."

It was Juliet's turn to hesitate, but then she smiled up at him as well and he could not help but kiss her. An action greatly approved of by both her maid and his valet, if their grins were anything to judge by. Nor did either object when told what James and Juliet had planned.

Indeed, the journey was surprisingly easy to arrange. Woods offered to travel to London to check on the question of a London town house and then meet them along the way. He was agreeable to the notion that he should take both the boy and the girl with him.

"Take them to Sir Thomas and Lady Levenger's house. I shall write a note for you to give them and I think they will be willing to have the pair. Later, when we return to London, Mrs. Langford will take charge of Abigail and I shall take charge of Daniel."

"Perhaps Margaret should go as well. We can manage together, you and I, until they join us," Juliet suggested. "It will look better if Abigail does not arrive simply in the company of men."

James nodded. "I must also write a note to the chaplain's assistant up at Dover Castle and I suppose I had best deliver it myself. But I shall be back within the hour," he promised Juliet. "Be ready to leave when I get back. It will be late to set out then but I should like to see how far we can go before dark. Dover is not, I think, the safest of places for us just at the moment."

"We shall be ready to go," Juliet promised.

"And I shall have the boy and girl ready to leave for London," Woods said. He permitted himself a thin smile. "I do not think they will object, either, to seeing the last of this town."

"And I shall not mind a quick trip back to London," the maid added. "The poor girl is that frightened of her father finding her and will be glad of my company, I should think."

If it was more than an hour before they were on their way, it was not much later. And then Juliet and James were alone together. The coachman had his orders and they rattled along at a shocking pace that was a relief to both of them.

They talked of a number of things but eventually their thoughts turned, almost at the same moment, to London and their plans for the future.

"We shall need," James said slowly, "some other way to account for my wealth than gambling. I should begrudge every moment I had to spend being seen at the gaming tables to support that nonsensical tale. And I should far rather spend such time with you."

Since these words were accompanied by a kiss to the palm of her hand, Juliet found herself blushing. "Nor should I like it," she said, "to have everyone say I drove you to the gaming tables by my shrewishness! Could you say, perhaps, that you had invested your previous winnings on the Exchange?"

James shook his head. "I could but I should rather not do so. Suppose it were to plunge? I should have to pretend that I had lost everything."

Juliet nodded. She was silent a moment then cautiously she said, "Could we say that I had brought a far larger portion to the marriage than had been supposed? I do not see how my parents could deny it without looking very odd."

"And perhaps," James said slowly, "we could also say that George had increased my allowance handsomely, now that I am a married man. He could not deny it without looking mean and having someone ask him why he had not."

They looked at one another, their eyes agleam with mischief. It was Juliet's smile that faltered first.

"How shall we go on?" she asked. "With the experiments and your inventions, I mean."

He understood. "I should be reluctant," he said, feeling his way, "to expose either of us to the ridicule and censure of those who would not approve of what we do. And yet we cannot stop."

"No, we cannot!" she echoed in shocked tones.

James smiled and kissed her hand again. "It is not just that we should suffer if we stopped," he explained. "But Harry may have need of our help again. Or even Philip for his mill. But there is a risk if any of Napoleon's supporters should guess at our work."

"So it is danger, not just censure you fear," she replied slowly.

He nodded. Juliet fell silent and waited, knowing that James knew the London world they would live in far better than she did. And she trusted him. Nor did he fail her.

"The boy. He is quick of mind and might make an excellent assistant. If so, he can oversee the work when we cannot be there. For there will be such times," James said.

"Even so," she added thoughtfully, "there will be occasions when we do not notice the time. How shall we explain our disappearances then?"

He stared at her a moment and then a smile, a mischievous smile, lit his face. "We could say," he told her with an air of innocence that deceived neither of them, "that we are unfashionably taken with one another. We will not need to explain further, for the imaginations of our listeners and the gossipmongers of the *ton* will supply all the rest of the explanation that might be needed."

"And it shall have the advantage of being at least in part the truth," she said, with the same air of spurious innocence. "We shall become the most frivolous couple in London and no one will suspect us of deeper things."

"I shall wear my most elaborate waistcoats," James said with a grin, "and perhaps even adopt a patch. Do you think a pale pink coat would be going too far? No one would think to take me seriously then."

"And I could wear all the frills I despise," Juliet countered with a grin of her own.

"There will not be anyone who thinks we have two thoughts to rub together between us!" James finished up the game.

They clasped hands in perfect accord. After a moment, however, Juliet's smile wavered a trifle. "I don't like being thought a fool and an antidote," she said.

He kissed her hand yet again. "No, nor I. But it will not be forever. Once this accursed war is over, it will not matter so greatly if people guess what we do. And you are, you will always be, beautiful to me."

And what was there to say to that? Juliet was not about to object to such flattery. She thought wistfully of the new gowns Mrs. Wise had made for her. Well, she would just have to wear them for James when they were alone together. Somehow the thought was not altogether unappealing.

"I shall be glad of the day when we need no longer pretend," she said with quiet sincerity. "I do not like the notion that either of us should pretend to be who we are not. I should rather set a fashion to encourage others to do what you have done, what we shall do together."

It was his turn to nod. "Perhaps," he suggested slowly, "we could begin by inviting one or two unusual thinkers to our house. And then more. We could hold salons and appear to become interested in science and mechanical things. Then, when the war is over, and thus the danger to us is also over, and it is safe for us to do so, we may begin to do our work more openly."

They smiled at one another then in perfect accord.

This, thought Juliet, was why she had fallen in love with the man and why, through all the years of their lives, she knew she would never tire of being married to him. How could she when he was the other half of her soul?

A moment later he startled her yet again.

"Why do you allow your family to distress you so?" he asked.

"Why do you let yours dictate what you will or will not allow society to know?" she countered.

He hesitated then smiled. "You are right, of course. We are kindred souls in that regard. But it need not continue to be that way."

"What do you mean?" she asked warily.

He frowned in that endearing way of his that had Juliet wanting to smooth the crease between his brows. "We plan, for reasons of our own, to continue to play the parts our families have decreed for us. But that does not mean that in private we must let them dictate to us so. We could begin to demand that my brother and your parents treat us with the respect we deserve."

"Do you actually believe they will listen?" Juliet asked doubtfully.

He smiled now and kissed her hand once again, thoroughly distracting her so that she almost missed his next words.

"I believe," he said with a firmness that warmed her, "we shall only find out if we try. We shall visit your home, and the moment your parents treat you with the least disrespect, we shall stop them. You are my wife and I will not tolerate such a thing."

He said it as though it were entirely his part to decide the matter, Juliet thought. What foolishness! But then, it would seem that even now her husband had a great deal to learn about her and about the whole notion of marriage. If he thought she would tamely allow him to fight all her battles for her, he

would soon find he was mistaken. Indeed, she planned
to fight a few on his behalf as well.

Harry's ship tossed on the rough water but he stood
as steady as if the water were smooth as glass. He was
going back to Spain. Back to Wellington and back to
the war. But his thoughts were on home. On his brothers, on their peaceful lives. He did not precisely envy
them, but neither could he prevent a twinge of something like that emotion.

Still, he had to be here. Something drove him, something he could not even name. Duty. Honor. They
were part of it, of course, but not the whole. All his
life he had known he had a destiny. Perhaps now it
was about to be fulfilled.

But that was too fanciful for the major and he
turned on his heel and went back below decks. Back
to where one of his fellow travelers needed his help.

In the depths of Dover Castle, two men slipped
through the tunnels. No one saw them go, no one
would notice their escape for several hours.

And in the town below there was a group of men
who were also making good their escape. "For there
is no knowing how soon they will lay information
against us," one said. "We'd best be gone afore they
do."

"It goes against the grain to leave," another
protested.

"P'r'aps. But I'd rather swallow me pride and leave
than be clapped up into jail. There be other towns
and other spots to do what we does best. And that's
summat we can't do if they catches us 'ere."

There was some grumbling, but even more nodding
of heads. And one by one they began to slip out of
the inn by the back way. Some would find new occupa-
tions. The others would meet up at the appointed spot

at the appointed time. And their work would begin anew farther up the coast.

Two days later, Juliet and James paused on the steps of her parents' home. "Are you certain you wish to be here?" he asked, concerned by her sudden pallor.

She nodded firmly, though it took her a moment to gather her courage to speak. "I must be here."

At his look of surprise, she went on, "All my life I thought I wished only to escape. To find a place where I could do the things I love. And now I have—with you. And I find that I wish to come back here. To face my parents on my own terms instead of theirs. I should not," she said, pausing to smile tremulously, "have the courage to do so were it not for you."

Troubled, James asked, "Was it so terrible a child-hood for you, then?"

"Terrible? No. Only lonely, I should say. Always believing there was something wanting, something wrong with me," she answered with a painful smile. "But with you I have found peace. I know that must sound fanciful, but it is the truth."

In answer, he kissed her hand. And then, holding it clasped firmly between his, he led her up the steps and into her parents' home.

Epilogue

～⌒～

James and George and Philip and Sir Thomas Levenger raised their glasses in a toast. Athenia sat stiffly by her husband's side, but Emily and Agatha and Juliet smiled at one another knowingly. Over the past year, Juliet had come to know them all well.

"To my brothers, who are finally settling down," George said.

"To young lovers," countered Sir Thomas Levenger.

"Like Lady Levenger and yourself," Philip added with an impudent grin.

"To life," James said simply.

"To the newest Langford!" Juliet said softly, looking down at Emily's child.

"To the next one to come," Emily countered, looking pointedly at Juliet's increasing middle. "It would seem the book was helpful?"

"What book?" Agatha asked, her eyes bright with interest.

With a glance to make certain the men were paying no attention, Emily grinned at her aunt and said softly, "Come, Juliet and I will show you."

Lady Darton watched them, patently torn. As they disappeared through the doorway, she rose to her feet and said to the men in her most austere voice, "I mistrust the levity in their voices. I had best go and see this book they were speaking of."

When Athenia was gone as well, George shook his head and raised his glass again. "To the ladies," he said, "none of whom will we ever be able to understand."

With amused glances, James and Philip and Sir Thomas raised their glasses as well. "I don't even try," Philip said solemnly.

James and Sir Thomas nodded. George appeared scarcely to have heard him. After a moment he said, "You know, speaking of libraries, it's deuced odd. I can't seem to find the Bible. The one our father had that was his pride and joy. I meant to write in the birth of Philip's son."

So intent was he on his own thoughts, that George did not even notice the alarmed look that passed between the others. He was somewhat surprised, however, when Philip turned the subject by speaking with rather more haste than was seemly. He said the only thing he could think of to distract his older brother.

"Odd? I shall tell you what is odd! You increasing James's allowance upon the event of his marriage and not increasing mine under the same circumstances."

Too late Philip realized that James was frantically trying to signal him. But he could not miss the astonished gaze George turned on both of them.

"Now that is another odd thing. Just lately, I have heard all over London that I did so and yet it is not true. I—"

But what he meant to say they never did find out because Sir Thomas immediately demanded, "Well, why the devil not? For both your brothers?"

"I, but, that is to say, Philip has a profession! He hasn't needed an allowance from me for some time," George retorted, offended. He glared at Philip. "You haven't received one since you inherited that tidy estate when you did. So what is this nonsense about anyway?"

He didn't wait for an answer but turned on his other

brother. "And you, James, did not ask me to increase your allowance either. You know very well I did not. Indeed, you gave me to understand that Miss Galsworth brought a more handsome settlement to the marriage than any of us knew. So I wish you will tell your brother so."

James held up his hands placatingly. "Please, none of this matters. Philip and I can contrive to manage as we are. But perhaps, George, it would be as well not to try to deny the rumor. That would only serve to keep it alive. And people might ask the same question Sir Thomas just did."

"Excellent advice," Philip agreed, a mischievous glint to his eyes. "One wouldn't want to be forever answering to those who would otherwise consider you a clutchfist."

"No, no, one wouldn't!" George said, nodding vigorously even as he blanched at the image conjured up by his brother's words.

Sir Thomas then managed to neatly turn the subject yet once again, this time by repeating the latest *on-dit* about a peer who unmistakably was clutchfisted.

James watched with patent satisfaction. He wondered, though, just what book it was that the ladies were off looking at. And why it had caused them such merriment. Eventually he went looking for Juliet to find out.

Juliet was in the library with Emily and her aunt Agatha and Athenia. They were all giggling together like schoolgirls. At the sight of James standing in the doorway, however, Philip's wife hastily thrust a book behind her and all four blushed becomingly. Juliet instantly rose and came to meet him, her spectacles still perched, charmingly in his opinion, on her nose.

There was a quiver in her voice that sounded suspiciously like suppressed laughter as she said, with none too convincing innocence, "Did you wish to speak to me, James?"

He did not at once answer her. He could not. His attention was caught too firmly by the curious way in which Athenia was avoiding his eyes. When she realized he was staring at her, she rose to her feet looking oddly unsteady, and said in a voice he had never heard her use before, "Tell me, James. Is George still with the others?"

He nodded, not trusting himself to speak. She smiled thinly and walked toward the doorway, swaying slightly in a manner that in any other woman he might have called seductive. But not Athenia! The notion was unthinkable.

Still, he could not help wondering just what the ladies had been doing, for he would swear there was a softness, a hint of something smoldering, in Lady Darton's eyes as she passed by him.

When she was gone and Juliet repeated her question, James managed to bring himself back to the present. He could not resist teasing his wife just a little. "I, er, thought it time I took my leave. That matter we were discussing on the way over. But there is no need for you to come, if you would prefer to stay."

"No need to come?" her eyes blazed with anger. "When it was my notion in the first place? You are very much mistaken, sir, if you think you can leave without me."

James chuckled and reached out to pull her close, oblivious to the interested eyes of Emily and Agatha and Athenia.

"Somehow I did not think you would let me do so," he said, placing a kiss on her forehead.

She smiled that shy smile that had become so dear to his heart. And he could not resist hugging her closer, even if it did dislodge her spectacles. How, he wondered, had he come to be such a fortunate fellow?

A discreet cough recalled them both to their circumstances, and James and Juliet hastily took their leave of everyone. A short time later their carriage was headed for the workshop.

"George was not to know, but Harry has sent word that the information my signal scheme sent across the channel has helped Wellington to win a major victory."

Juliet squeezed his arm. "I am so glad!" she said fiercely. "I hope this dreadful war will soon be over and Harry safely restored to you."

Only the way the corners of his mouth tightened betrayed the depth of James's own emotions. And the curtness of his nod as he acknowledged her words. Truth be told, he was glad to pull the carriage to a halt at the workshop and not have to put into words how he felt.

Inside they found Daniel, the boy rescued in Dover. Except that he was rapidly becoming a young man, a very useful one, and at the moment he was grinning. "I've done it, sir," he said.

Moments later, all else was forgotten as three heads pored over the latest experiment. Somehow it was a fitting way, Juliet thought, to celebrate the first anniversary of her marriage to James. Though mind, she did have other plans for later, for when they were back home again.

Looking at the book with Emily and Athenia and Lady Levenger had reminded her of some of the things she had not yet had the chance to try. And there was, after all, that very special night shift Abigail had made for her under Mrs. Wise's direction. It was so sheer one could almost see through the fabric and Juliet smiled to herself at the thought of James's reaction when he saw her wearing it.

The expression on her face was quite sufficient to make James decide to hurry, just a bit. For the first time in his life he had the sense, these days, that his experiments could wait, that there might be other things that mattered more. Such as his smiling wife.

Daniel perhaps said it best when he told them scornfully, "Yer ought to go home and come back in the morning. Billing and cooing as ye are, yer attention ain't on things here."

Somehow they could not find the heart to disagree.

Author's Note

Look for Harry's story in *The Sentimental Soldier.* What happens when Harry literally stumbles across a young woman who is where she ought not to be? He can and will protect her from everyone—except perhaps himself.

Look for news of upcoming books at my website: http://www.sff.net/people/april.kihlstrom

I love hearing from readers. I can be reached by E-mail at: april.kihlstrom@sff.net
Or write to me at: April Kihlstrom
Suite 240
532 Old Marlton Pike
Cherry Hill, NJ 08053

Please send an SASE for a newsletter and reply.

Fair Game by Diane Farr

A young woman of unearthly beauty. Her unscrupulous mother. A powerful womanizer demanding repayment of a large debt. All amount to a most peculiar sojourn in the country, a tangle with a hat pin, and a shocking barter that leaves everyone fair game....

0-451-19856-5/$4.99

The Magic Jack-O'-Lantern by Sandra Heath

A heartbroken—and invisible—brownie hitches a ride with an angelic heiress...and brings his mischievous brand of Halloween chaos to high society. The problem is, the pompous Sir Dominic Fortune does not believe in such superstitions...until the magic of love makes his heart glow brighter than a jack-o'-lantern.

0-451-19840-9/$4.99

To order call: 1-800-788-6262